THE WRITER AND HIS WIFE
AND OTHER STORIES

THE WRITER AND HIS WIFE
AND OTHER STORIES

RABINDRANATH MAHARAJ

PEEPAL TREE

First published in Great Britain in 1996
Peepal Tree Press Ltd.
17 King's Avenue
Leeds LS6 1QS
Yorkshire
England

© Rabindranath Maharaj 1996

All rights reserved
No part of this publication
may be reproduced or transmitted
in any form without permission

ISBN 0 948833 81 5

CONTENTS

The Librarian	7
The Writer and His Wife	22
Dirty River	35
The Minister of Ancillary Units	51
Clouds	74
The Metalwork Technician	83
The Funeral	97
John Fitzgerald Tennyson	122
Heading for the Cold	155
Designs	163
The Occasional Sadhu	171

In memory of my brother Darin

THE LIBRARIAN

He had been a librarian for over ten years but now he was disillusioned with his work. All his friends, those who had begun to work in the library with him, had left. Some were teachers, a few had migrated to Canada, and others had become public relations officers and advertising agents. There were even a few insurance salesmen. Things were so bad that Bashir Ali, who had risen to the position of Senior Librarian at the Princes Town Branch, would become very agitated whenever a new trainee came. He would look at the way they handled the books, their method of cataloguing, the time spent in reading rather than in re-arranging the magazines. And it pained him to know that these budding librarians would soon move on to greener pastures, while he, Bashir, would stay.

There was a time when he had revelled in his role as a librarian. He had felt then a quiet, secret kinship with the writers and viewed himself as a specially chosen custodian of their works. Sometimes the relationship became even more intimate. During the early mornings, when the library was still empty, he would produce a gold embellished, hard-cover edition of Dostoevsky and gaze fondly at the cover. Then with tremulous hands he would allow the pages to slip through his fingers. He would shake his head.

'Ah Fydor,' he would say; 'nobody read you this week. Nobody appreciates you.' And in his mind he would complete the sentence. 'No one except Bashir.'

Sometimes, at the end of a particularly tiring day when he was replacing the books on the shelves, he would come across a book in the West Indian section.

'Ah Vidiadhar, so much problems we have. Them Tulsis too damn fast. Chut man!' Then he would give a little self-deprecating laugh, startling those who had entered to borrow or return a book before the library closed its doors.

So perhaps the reputation that he had garnered over the years was not totally unwarranted. He, in turn, aware of the snickers, the stifled giggles of the school girls, became even more sensitive about his job.

'Quiet!' he would shout across the room, his voice trembling with rage. This is a library not a parlour!'

'Ah Leo,' he would say to himself, 'this world is peopled with callous, uncaring deviants.'

He knew all about borrowers. He could predict at a minute's glance who would mistreat the books; those who would fling them idly on the table or on the floor. He would peer sternly over his spectacles at everyone who had come to borrow a book. The school-children would fidget uneasily under his grim appraisal while others, who were late for work, would steups loudly. But Bashir was not to be daunted.

Those who had come to return books were subject to an even more meticulous appraisal. He could tell by smelling the pages the type of treatment the book had received over the last few days. He would look at the frayed spine and know that the covers had been bent back while the reader lay on his bed, or smell the sharp, sanitised odour and realise that it had been read in the lavatory.

At times he could not contain his anger. 'Bhagi and rice! You put bhagi and rice on top of Virginia! You think Virginia like bhagi and rice so much that you have to offer it to her? All you blasted Indian from the country could never appreciate anything. Never-Never!'

Once a taxi-driver, returning a manual on auto-mechanics, had abused him rather badly. 'Who the hell you calling illiterate! If wasn't for these kiss-me-ass little children here I woulda...'

As the taxi-driver was leaving he said, 'Saying that he could smell carburettor spray all over the book. Mr. Great Smeller!' He slammed the door.

Bashir was shaken by this and became more selective about passing judgement. For a few days afterwards he kept a sharp lookout, but the taxi-driver never returned.

It was after incidents like these that a thick wall of depression encircled him and he would feel like an innocent prisoner condemned to a life sentence.

He would lie tossing on his bed, considering his ill luck. The words would form in his mind: Will my life end up like yours, Edgar, derelict, dazed, wandering here and there and finding no solace from anyone? He would draw his heel away from the hard, protruding end of the bed, up towards the thin sheet of foam that he had placed over the wooden boards. Then he would place his palms over his knees, massaging the thin, knobbly joints. Sometimes he would fall asleep like this. When he awoke his hands would still be on his knees and slowly and painfully he would straighten his legs.

He lived alone and never slept with the lights off. Whenever he awoke in the middle of the night, he would survey the unpainted walls, looking at the lizards carefully secreted in the cracks and then jumping out, trapping a moth or butterfly. He would look at the insect's diminishing convulsions in the lizard's mouth and then he would close his eyes tightly, trying to force sleep to overwhelm him.

'Quoth the Raven, Never more,' he would repeat again and again until the words ceased and only the echo remained to taunt him. 'Poor Bashir,' he would say. 'Poor, unlucky Bashir.'

But all of this was to change, even though it was not apparent at the beginning.

She came just when he had finished sorting out a list of errant borrowers, those who had refused to return their books even after two or three warnings.

Yes?' he said, looking up at her and tapping back his spectacles over the ridge of his nose.

'This is my first job.'

He did not immediately understand. When he understood, he looked at her more carefully. He saw the bobbed hair falling just over the ear, curling towards her cheeks. He frowned. He had always associated short hair in a female with licentiousness. The frown deepened as he examined the tight jersey and the faded denim trousers. Then he saw the lowered hands, clasping and unclasping. He looked at the face again, at the slightly upturned lips, at the eyes looking out questioningly at him. He wanted suddenly to speak with authority, with graceful power.

'What is your name?' he asked abruptly.

'Denyse. That's spelled with a 'y' not an 'i'.'

He smiled. 'That must be very important to you.'

She seemed flustered. 'No... it's just a name... how I've always spelled it.'

He took off his spectacles, casually tapping them against a book on the table. Then he remembered the dark circles under his eyes and hastily replaced the spectacles. He motioned her to a nearby chair. 'Come and sit here.'

She sat down, the legs slightly parted, the feet stretched before her. His uneasiness returned.

'What do you know about the Dewey cataloguing system?' he asked sternly
'Nothing, really.'
Ah! I see. And who going to teach you?'
'I dunno... You, I suppose.'
'And who going to see about the library while I teaching you?'
'Both of us.'
Both of us. He liked the sound of that. 'How old are you?'
'Twenty-one.'
'And how old you think I am?'
She looked at him, laughing. 'About thirty-six I suppose.'
He winced. 'I am twenty-nine years of age,' he said. 'And do you know when I started working here? When I was eighteen years. Packing away the books, dusting the shelves, repairing the damaged covers...'
'I will have to do all that too?'
'Well it depends.'
'Depends upon what?'
'Depends upon how efficient you are,' he said. 'Now tell me, how long you intend to work here?'
'Well it depends.'
'Upon what?'
'Upon how efficient you are,' she said laughing.
That night he massaged his knees, wiping his moist palms against the thin pajama cloth.
The next morning he cleaned the bedroom mirror with a damp towel. He saw his receding hairline and adjusted his hair downwards. He remembered a body-builder's pose that he had seen in a book in the library and flexed his biceps. His arms, like the rest of his body were long and thin. He observed his prominent Adam's apple and watched it disappear when he swallowed. Trying to see how long he could keep it hidden, he ended up in a fit of coughing.

For the next few days the other passengers in the taxi would say to him, 'Aye Bashir, how you deck off so?' or 'But Bashir man, how you smelling so sweet? Like you pick up something?' He had always hated this familiar, almost intimate tone. He would immerse himself in a book, trying to shut off the voices. Then he would hear someone say 'But Bashir, why you reading and studying so hard? Is time for you to get married, man, not waste your time in all them book.'

Inevitably someone would add, 'And how you sure that he don't have a little chick hide away behind all them shelf in the library?' Everyone except Bashir would laugh.

But the main beneficiary of this change was the library. In a short time, he had re-arranged it completely. The Girls' Romance Series, which he had always viewed with distaste, and which held a special fascination for the throngs of school girls who came in the library after school, were placed on the lower, more accessible shelves. Previously, he had arranged these books on the highest shelves where only he could stretch his long limbs to reach them. He cut out colourful pictures of athletes, dancers and movie-stars from old magazines and arranged them on eye-catching strips of cardboard placed at various points in the library Best of all, he would spend hours discussing and appraising these renovations with Denyse. He was surprised at how comfortable he felt with her.

'I like that chart over there,' he would say, 'The one with the moon touching the edge of the branch. Like if it want to kiss it.' There would be a little giggle and she would say, 'A moon kissing a tree. What stupidness!'

'No-no', he would say intently. 'Is not stupidness at all. A kiss don't have to be a bad thing or something rude. All these great poets use it to symbolise some special feeling. Is like if I just lean over and kiss you. You would find that rude?'

She would never reply; her smile sheathed in ambiguity.

One day he asked her, 'Why you always talking to that bunch of girls on that table?'

'Well, when I have nothing else to do...'

'You could talk to me for instance.'

'You? If we talk to each other all the time we would get bored.'

'You mean *you* will get bored. Not me.' After a while he asked, 'So what all you does be talking about so?'

'About things that girls talk to each other about.'

'I hope you all don't talk about me', he said, trying to sound casual.

'Sometimes.'

'And what they say?'

'Well, you know, the things that girls say.'

'Like what for instance?'

'Like how they never see you dress up so before.'

'And anybody ever explain why this might be so?'

'Yeah. Everybody.'

'And you?'

'And me what?'

'What you think is the reason for me dressing up like this. C'mon, don't laugh. You always laughing at everything. That is the way you does laugh with your boyfriend?' he asked, with sudden interest.

'No. We have better things to do.'

'He must be very happy.'

'He was.'

'He was what?'

'He was very happy. Like that little boy in that chart across there. You believe that! Balancing on that bicycle on just one wheel.'

'I had a tricycle once,' he said solemnly. 'Then my father took it away after I had ridden it only two or three times. I was afraid to ask him afterwards for it.' He took off his spectacles, not worrying about the dark hollows this time. 'That was always my problem. I could never ask for anything that I want. And in any case, nobody never give me anything.' Briefly he felt this sudden need to humiliate himself before her. 'That is why I possess nothing. No parents. No relatives, no nothing. Just the little, leaking cubicle that I live in.'

'Well, everybody pass through these phases', she said lightly.

'Phases? That is not a phase. That is my entire life! But I have very simple needs,' he said, relaxing. 'Look at this library here. For the last ten years or so this has been my life. Everything that I want and everything that I need. But what you think is the most valuable thing in this library to me now?' His eyes flickered at her, the dark circles narrowing.

'The encyclopaedia set?'

He shook his head.

'Then it must be the book on Victorian fashions.'

He observed her laughter, her upturned lips, the lack of any clear intent in her voice. 'I think we will close the library an hour earlier today. The weatherman say to expect plenty rain.'

That afternoon, just before he boarded a taxi, he went into a nearby pharmacy and bought an expensive retractable razor and ten shining blades. Just before he paid the cashier he tested one of the blades against his finger and was surprised to see the blood spurting out. He quickly thrust the injured finger into the pocket of his trousers, allowing the blood to leak within the inner lining. He looked around furtively but no one had seen.

During the early hours of the morning, he prepared himself. There was an almost ritualistic element in the way he went about his preparation. Setting up the stool next to the bed facing the mirror. Hanging the towel carefully on a nail at the side of his wardrobe and then positioning himself with so much solicitude on the stool.

He looked at this reflection in the mirror as if he would be seeing himself for the last time and then made a bold, downward stroke with the razor. He gazed in astonishment at the clean swathe that the blade had made, cleaving through the prickly hair and leaving a path like a newly-constructed, muddy road. He wondered whether he was doing the right things. Too late, he thought, and concentrated on the blade's downward thrusts. When he was finished he gazed with consternation at his face. Everything that the beard had hidden or camouflaged — the sunken cheeks, the prominent cheekbones, the slightly protruding teeth, the prominent Adam's apple — was exposed.

His consternation turned into alarm when he observed the greenish pallor the shaven portion of his face had acquired.

He felt naked. As in the dreams when he would be sitting behind the desk, stamping and cataloguing the books and then peering down and seeing his naked body. These were always dreams of shame and transgression.

Surveying his reflection, he thought that he looked like a unripe orange, hastily peeled, the greenish tinge blending in with the pale yellow. Then his gaze fell upon the protruding upper teeth and he saw instead some poor, trapped opossum.

'Oh God, Bashir!' he shrieked aloud. 'What you do to yourself?'

He chose an empty taxi and tried to hide his face with a newspaper. Then someone noticed.

'Aye everybody. Look they pluck Bashir!'

'What happen, Bashir man? Like you fall in a plucking machine?'

'And look how green-green he face looking!'

The taxi-driver adjusted his rear-view mirror, every now and again, taking a surreptitious look at Bashir, chuckling silently.

Bashir's face sank deeper into the newspaper. He swallowed and tried to lock his throat into that position, trying to cut off his supply of air. He thought of the next day's newspaper headline:

Librarian with Defective Adam's Apple Suffocates in Taxi!

In the library, he acted as though nothing had happened. He went straight to his desk and began filing away the cards. He did this very quickly; his fingers selecting a card and then placing it into an open drawer. He continued for about thirty minutes, never looking up, not missing a card. Drawers were opened and slammed shut, cards neatly arranged in their proper places. When he found that the sweat made his shirt cling to his skin, he stopped. And looked up.

He saw a boy chewing gum, flicking through a book idly and glancing at a girl at the next table. He surveyed the entire length of the rectangular building. He saw the colourful charts and the boy riding on the tricycle. He saw the dishevelled shelf where he had placed the Girls' Romance Series. He observed the walls, the ceiling, the half-empty trolley placed near a shelf. He saw the sets of encyclopaedia that were probably over twenty years old and considered how much useless and obsolete information had passed into the hands of students and researchers. He realised for the first time how much the library looked like an old government building that had its internal walls removed. They had not even bothered to repaint the building, he thought. Nor install a proper ventilation system. He looked at the old iron fan just above his head, spinning so slowly that it had allowed some type of wasp to construct a small muddy-looking nest. The cobwebs on the rafters. The dust that had settled on the filing cabinet and on the higher shelves. No wonder he was turning green, spending his time in a place like this. He remembered how he had looked in the mirror that morning. Like an opossum. Like an opossum that was stupid enough to believe it could be something else. A poor, trapped animal working in a library. Library? More like a mortuary for dead books.

Librarians probably grew to look like undertakers. He'd never really seen an undertaker, except perhaps in movies, but the image stiffened in his mind : tall, narrow, angular. After a while other adjectives suggested themselves: gaunt, insipid, lifeless. His fingers trembled. He thought: We have evolved separately; a completely different species. All these years of stretching for books, surrounded by them, breathing in all their deceitful germs. Doomed from the beginning.

But was he not the specially chosen custodian entrusted with the writings of all his dear friends? Was he not special, someone set apart? Someone who had dedicated his entire life to his work?

To what end? The thought came to him just like that; unsolicited. He was surprised at first. To what end? He repeated it several times in his mind, waiting for an unsolicited answer.

He heard a calypso being played in a cafeteria some distance away. The voice became clearer, the words more distinct, until he could actually distinguish entire stanzas. He had walked past this cafeteria every day, and knew that its owner continually played calypsos and reggae. Yet, in the library he had never been aware of this.

And then he heard cars outside honking their horns, the screeching of tyres. He saw the boy still chewing gum, still casting sidelong glances at the girl and felt the jagged edge of the boy's intention, obscene and revolting, enter his mind.

He looked up. Someone was standing before him. He could not contain his rage.

'Why the hell you want to borrow that book for? You think Gabriel write that book especially for you? So you could just come in here and pick it up and walk away with it! What you know about Gabriel?' he shouted, standing now. 'You think he went through all the pain and suffering to write that book only for you?' The boy dropped the book on the desk and ran out of the library.

It took him most of the morning to compose himself. When she came, bright-eyed and energetic, he was reading a magazine.

'Sorry to be so late,' she said.

'Oh. Is okay.'

'You mean... I thought you might be vexed.' Then she focused on his face. 'What happen to the beard?'

'The face was tired of it. And how *your* face so red?'

'I was hurrying to get down here. But you look so different, Bashir, without that beard. I probably wouldn't even recognise you in a crowd.'

'Sometimes we don't even recognise the most important thing.'

'But what cause you to shave it off?'

'Because I felt like it.'

'I didn't know that you was so impulsive.'

'What you know about me?' he asked, as if he had suddenly grown tired.

'I know that you enjoy your work very much.'

'Is that all?'

'I know that you've read most of the books here. And that you are irritated by carelessness. And the school girls find you funny and sometimes think that you are mad.' She hesitated. 'And that you find me interesting.'

'Interesting?' He considered the word, not sure of what she meant.

'Yeah. Like, you know, you find me attractive.' She saw the slight, nervous tremor pass through his hands.

'But... I never gave any indication to you that...' He was unsure of what to say. 'Are you making fun of me?' he asked, looking at her face.

'Don't you find me attractive?'

He became silent for a while. Then he said, 'I am thinking of leaving the library.'

She sat down beside him, stretching her legs in her nonchalant manner.

'Where will you go?'

'Oh. I don't know. Migrate. Become an insurance salesman.'

'Just like the others you told me about?'

'Perhaps they were the smart ones.'

'But you love this place. You always said so.'

He listened to her, trying to detect any note of pleading in her voice. Even when she was serious, there was this barely perceptible hint of laughter about her.

'You really serious?' she asked.

He nodded.

After a while she said, 'I hope that I didn't have anything to do with it.'

The anger he was trying to contain, came again.

'You compliment yourself.' He saw the confusion in her face and momentarily felt the need to hurt her. 'You... just some little girl...'

'I didn't mean...'

'When I make any decision, I make them with only me in mind. Nobody influences me to do what I want to do. Nobody. Least of all you. Why do you think that you could ever be so important as to influence my decision?'

'You look very strange without that beard,' she said abruptly.

'Like an orange?'

'No. Like some kind of animal. A ferret? I'm not sure.'

'An opossum,' he said, without any bitterness now. 'A manicou. People shoot them all the time.'

'But you look nice, in a different sort of way.'

'I thought you said "was".'

"Was what?"

"Was happy.'

Then she understood. 'He came to my house this morning. Said he wanted to talk. I was thinking of not going at first, then I decided that it couldn't do any harm.'

'Did it?'

She clasped her hands behind her neck, sliding down the chair a bit. 'It depends on whose point of view you looking from.'

'Let's say, from my point of view.'

She unclasped her fingers and began twirling the hair that fell in a semicircle over her cheek. He thought she was going to laugh. Instead, she said, 'He came to tell me about this job in Port of Spain.'

He saw then that there was no need to ask, 'I hope you enjoy the job,' he said.

She bent down and took off a slipper, adjusting a strap. Her hand brushed his leg. She replaced the slipper and sat up. 'Is about closing time. I suppose I should leave now.' As she walked away, she hesitated by the doorway. Then she was gone.

Bashir Ali did not become an insurance salesman. Nor did he migrate. What he did was write letters. To Government departments. To charitable organisations. And to businesses. In a few months the library was repainted and an annex constructed to accommodate the recent sets of encyclopaedia and hard-cover books that had been acquired. When he travelled to work in the taxi, the other passengers would say, 'Bashir man, you really have that library looking spic-and-span', or, 'Just this morning I was telling me son that if he want to pass he exam and come a lawyer he have to spend at least one day a week in the library. One day at least.' And when he had alighted from the taxi, they would say, 'That Bashir fella really make out of gold. Just imagine, he dedicate he whole life to that library. Always writing letter and collecting money to buy this and build that.'

Later in the day, resting back on his swivelling chair behind his shining, new desk, surveying the fan rotating so quickly and yet making no sound, he would say, 'Ah Friedrich. What more can I ask for? I was right from the very beginning. I was always cut out to be a librarian. Nobody could take that from me. Nobody. As long as I am here, nobody could do anything to you all. My job is to protect and serve. Just like the police.' Then, with his eyes closed, he would tenderly place his fingers on the cover of a book and make low, pleasurable, grunting sounds.

THE WRITER AND HIS WIFE

'I going to write that book you know boy, I going to write that book soon.'

Once I had asked him, 'What the book going to be about?'

He had replied, 'About everything I ever thought of since I born.'

They, relatives of my parents, would come almost every weekend.

She would be the first to leave the car, slamming the door, not looking back. He, almost in deference, would remain in the car for a minute or two, winding up the glass, testing the handbrakes, fixing the car-mat. Then, when she had entered our house, he would open the door of the car and stand around, waiting for someone to invite him in or until his wife shouted, 'Come here Roop. Nobody going to thief the car.'

She was the most powerful woman I had ever seen. Fat perhaps, but with the fat so evenly proportioned over her biceps, her neck, her legs, that she looked like a retired female wrestler.

It always surprised me when she called him Roop – his complete name was Roopnarine – it was the only term of endearment that she ever used.

Once, when I was about six years or so, I had visited their house. They had owned a gas station and she was in the yard, quarrelling with a gas pump attendant.

Roop was in the service room, carefully filing away bills in an old, grey folder.

'This is hard work you know, boy. You have to keep everything in your head, in case you misplace this folder.'

Then he had produced a red, dusty notebook from beneath some older newspapers. 'You see this? This is where I going to write a book. A important book.' He blew some dust off the covers and then replaced the notebook beneath the newspapers. It was the first time I can remember him speaking about writing the book.

There is one more memory of that visit. Their son, older than I, offering to show me how the pump worked and then, pointing the nozzle at my feet, filling my shoe with the gas.

She had seen. 'This Aiknath always wasting gas. Look how careless he is.'

I remember seeing him through the glass doors of the station, adjusting his folders, pretending that he had not seen.

On our way home my mother said, 'What smelling so? Don't tell me you start drinking gas now. What happen, pitch-oil too cheap for you?'

I remember them too at the time my grandfather died. The body had just been placed in the hearse. I was standing at the side of the road, watching relatives, most of whom I had never seen before, imploring the driver of the hearse.

'Why you carrying him away for? Why you doing that?'

'Oh God! He never do you anything. He never do anybody anything. And now you want to take him away.'

Another relative was holding onto a mirror on the door, wringing and massaging. 'You never know people would have treat you so, eh Pundit? You was too good to think so.'

The driver of the hearse was surveying everything impassively, no doubt he was accustomed to such scenes.

Afterwards, when most of the relatives had reluctantly departed, they had remained. She was in the yard telling my father, 'Life so strange. One minute you whistling like a bird and the next minute you foot up in the air.'

Aiknath was rummaging through a pile of flowers, searching for coins. She had said, 'Move away from they, Aik, or the old man will lock you neck tonight.' He ran to her, nestling under her massive arm.

I was sitting on a rented chair, looking at the tent that had been constructed two days earlier. Roop came and sat next to me.

'Life is like that, you know,' he had said solemnly. 'Who could say no when the great one above call up one of his servant. Sometimes is better, you know. No more suffering. No more pain.'

I realised that he was trying to offer solace. I nodded, looking at the bamboo posts that supported the canvas of the tent.

'Life is a funny thing,' he said. 'But whatever happen to us, it's God who will it so. We are helpless driftwood cast in the sea of destiny, in the ocean of fate; the tides going and coming are like the little joys and problems that confront us. Sometimes the ocean is filled with pollution and sometimes it is pure and unblemished.' His eyes acquired a glazed look. He shook his head. 'We are more than the fireflies and less than the fireflies.'

He did not explain. I looked at the faces of my uncles, trying to understand what they were feeling. Sitting on a chair, listening to him, I awaited sorrow and grief; but felt only guilt.

'Change is inevitable,' he continued. 'Everything is always changing, so why should we deny it? Look around you. Look at the breeze blowing through the crepe paper. Look at the dog wagging its tail. Even now we are changing, breathing in tiny little microbes and germs that are nibbling away at our privates.

By privates I mean organs. So why resist it? Even the earth itself is always rotating and the universe is in a state of constant agitation.'

Aiknath, now trapped under his mother's arm, was wriggling and twisting, trying to lever the arm upwards and away. She was quite unaware of his efforts, her legs planted like two massive Grecian pillars. An uncle, seeing his discomfort, called out to him. She raised her arm and he bounded out, as if released from a slingshot.

'Take care that dog bite you, Aik. Look how thin and mangy it is. You will sure get rabies. G'wan dog. Mash!' She stamped her feet. The dog looked at her and fled.

'That dog has experienced change. She is just the agent of that change.'

He never called her by any name; even now I can't recollect what her first name might have been. (My younger brother always referred to her as 'the Battleship' and the name had stuck. He would scream with genuine terror whenever he saw her. 'Look! Look the Battleship reach!' Then he would run to the back of the house.)

He was examining the folds of his trouser, removing pieces of lint.

'So what I was, in effect, speaking about is that sometimes a storm may hurl us hither and thither, and sometimes this same storm will deposit us peacefully on some tropical island.'

His wife called out then. 'Come, Roop. Bring you tail across here.' Then she said to my father, but loud enough for all to hear, 'Sometimes I feel that Roop didn't design too correct. Like if some screw missing or cross-thread.'

'But until that time,' he continued sadly, 'we have to just ride with the tide. Not questioning our helplessness, but seeing it as part of some larger design. Think of how sweeter then the fruits will taste,' he had said without much conviction.

Just before I left, he said, 'I have to register all these thoughts, you know, boy. I have to record them soon, before they are plucked away from me.'

Then the gas station was repossessed. The bank put it into the hands of a receiver who auctioned it off. A few days later, we heard that the station had been purchased by a close relative, one of her and my father's cousins. The purchasing family, the Seepauls, were very wealthy and lived in a very prestigious section of San Fernando, called Seepaul Lands. As they had grown wealthier, they had stopped fraternising. They would come to the prayers and functions, but depart early. But what was most galling in the eyes of the relatives was the way they refused to be drawn into taking sides in family squabbles.

For the few months afterwards she was livid. Her hand, so devoid of muscle and yet so powerful, was the clearest demonstrator of her anger. It would jiggle with unrestrained rage. It would come down crashing on the table. It would encircle Aiknath with so much force that his cheeks would redden and his eyes bulge.

'And them nasty bitches have the guts to call themself family. Family!' She looked as though she was going to utter some obscenity 'Waiting like corbeaux to take what they could get. That is why everybody in that family so blight. The father so old and dry up like a salt prunes. And all the family take after him. Excepting Anthony,' she said. 'He like a bison. I don't know why they don't rent him out to a breeding unit in the Agriculture Station. The big, fat, lazy thing. And he so duncy. That is why they had to send him to a private school in the town to do some kind of computer and typewriting course. A big, blasted, hardback man doing typewriting! Is no wonder they always hiding-hiding inside the house. Feeling they too good for anybody else. The last time I gone they, you know what they offer me? Ice-cream! I could have pelt the ice-cream right back in they face. Ask Aik what I do to him afterwards for not refusing to take the ice-cream. Eh, Aik? You remember the licks you get? The ungrateful wretches and them.'

Once she told my father, 'Is that blasted bad-knob daughter they have that cause everything. She friendly with the bank manager who twice she age. That is how they was the first to know that the property was mortgaged and that we had a small, little problem. You see how they does plot and scheme? All of them is one set of conniving bitches. One day when Roop driving and I spot them on the road, I will just lean across and grab the steering and ram they motherass. Kill all of them one time.'

If the loss of the gas-station brought an unrelenting anger to her, he became even more enmeshed in his fatalism. Sometimes when her anger was terrible to behold, when she spewed her malice with so much expertise and relish, he would draw away, casting furtive little glances at her.

One Sunday morning I had brought them a bag of oranges that I had picked. She called out, 'Come Roop. Put this in the trunk.' He had come hurriedly, holding the bag away, afraid that it might dirty his white shirt. He always wore white shirts, buttoned at the cuffs and his trousers were always neatly creased.

'You making provision for the next life, you know,' he said. 'Everything that you give, you will get back ten times more in the following life. If you continue giving oranges like this you will be reborn as a...,' he hesitated, passing his hand over his oiled hair, 'yes, you will be a swami, living by yourself, deep in the forest. With no noise, no gas-station, no children, no family. Only the animals curling up by your feet. Waiting for you to stroke them before they go to sleep.' After a while, he said, 'Not like the Seepauls though. They would return as something less than human. Perhaps some lower kind of animal life. What is the type of bird that does steal from people house?'

Remembering a story, I said, 'A magpie.'

He smiled, the lines around his eyes and on his forehead deepening. 'Yes. Yes. A magpie. They would all be magpies.' He glanced at his wife as if a sudden thought had come to him. You know, I make a study of this reincarnation business. I could just look at somebody like that and know what they would be re-born into. Like she for instance. You think you could tell what she would be in the next life?' Herds and flocks and packs of animals cascaded in the air. Hippos and rhinos. Water buffaloes. And then mythical beasts. I imagined an overweight dragon, puffing out hate and flames from its nostrils. These thoughts brought a smile to me. He noticed.

'You know I feel that in plenty ways we think alike. That is why I always wanted you to be the first to know about this book. And guess what? It going to have a special section on reincarnation. I going to trace back until the first days of mankind. And then before that, when only plants used to live. You ever look at a fern carefully? They used to be among the first plants.' Then he looked worried. 'But is the grass that giving me problems. I can't figure out how, when all these millions of grass die, they does return as human being and animals. Where they does find so much human being and animal to re-born as?'

'Perhaps they re-born as other grass,' I said.

He considered that for a minute. 'Yes. I see your point. The little knot-grass will come back as something like a corn tree. And then, maybe a cherry tree, and then an orange tree and sometimes an apple tree. Yes. Yes. Very good. Even among the plants you have this scale. From lower to higher.' Then the worried look returned. 'But what about the microbes? The germs that does be nibbling away at your privates.' He shook his head disconsolately. 'I don't know what to say. Sometimes the more answers I find, the more questions arise. This world is a hard,

hard place and is thinkers like me who have the task of finding all the answers. This is why I does be thinking so much. And then I does hear little voices up here.' He tapped his head.

I remembered what she had told my father about his missing screws.

He said: 'In any case though, I not afraid of these voices. They here to help me. You know it had this great poet from Ireland who say that spirits used to write all his poetry.' The mournful look returned. 'But my spirits either too lazy or they not creative enough. No matter how much I try to force them, they never write a single line yet.'

'They can't be poetic spirit,' I said.

It seemed as though he was deliberating upon the comment. He said slowly, as if a revelation was asserting itself, bit by bit. 'You mean like if is a mathematical spirit? Or a spirit that more partial to science and now trapped in the mind of a philosopher? So then you could never have harmony. But this... this could be a dangerous thing! Like if you give somebody a different type of blood, the whole body will react against it. Then, this headache, the pain in my elbows and knees....'

When he returned some weeks later, he said, 'They gone.'

I asked him, 'The spirits?'

He replied, 'Just like that. They just move on.'

During the next few years I hardly ever saw them. I was attending a secondary school in San Fernando and during that time I stayed by another relative who lived close to the school. I remember, though, the night before I left. Most of my bags were already packed and my mother was searching for some ancient family good-luck charm to give to me. My younger brother was looking on at the pile of new books splayed out on the bed, tracing his fingers over the shiny covers.

I felt *her* heavy hand on my shoulder. 'You is a big man now, eh? Going off to live in San Fernando. But don't do like Vishram,' she said, referring to an uncle, 'and end up in the gambling pool all the time. You father and mother making a big sacrifice for you. The rest is up to you... Now you have the chance to go to a good school and make all the family proud.' She glanced angrily at Aiknath. 'I don't know why this blockhead didn't take after his mother side of the family.' She looked towards the books on the bed. My brother saw her approaching and ran off. She picked up an atlas, examining the binding, testing the covers. I became alarmed. Then she flung it back on the bed. 'Jagraphy.' she said.

He waited until she had started to speak to my father. Then he said, 'So you going off to college now. You mustn't waste this opportunity because the school you going to is a very good one. In that place they don't try to change you or make you learn things that are different from your own culture. That was the very same school that I wanted to go to but destiny thought otherwise. However, now is your time and you have to make the best use of it. Don't let anybody lead you astray and any spare-time you get, spend it in the school library. It will serve you well in life. Always remember that. Just now you will be too educated for me to give you advice but even though I didn't go to college, I always read a lot. That is why I could be in this position today,' he said softly, as if he was afraid that she might hear.

When they were leaving she said, 'And don't do no stupid typewriting subjects, eh.'

The next time I spoke to him was on the day prior to my marriage. I had seen neither him nor his wife for more than fifteen years and I was surprised at their appearances. She had discarded her silver-rimmed spectacles and now wore ones with a heavy plastic frame. Her yellowish skin looked unhealthy and there were tiny reddish spots all over her face and on her neck.

Her hands still retained some of their power, but now the flesh drooped unnaturally, creating the illusion of two arms joined somewhere at the shoulders. Yet from afar, she looked as formidable as ever. And this was the impression that lingered.

'Just yesterday you was a little bare-bottom boy running about in the yard and now you going to be married. I hope you getting into the right thing. Everybody nowadays quick to get married and the next thing you know they single again. I don't know what happening to all the young people now. Thank God Aiknath married into a good family.' I had seen him earlier on the arms of his robust wife and, at that instant, all of the dislike that I had harboured for years, just vaporised.

'You must always remember,' she said, 'to show her who is the boss from early on. Don't be afraid to slam she around a little bit... Otherwise it will be she who will end up driving the carriage and you with four legs on the road. That is something I always admire Roop for, he was never afraid to put down his foot. Don't mind that I was a little rough sometimes, but I always know that he was the boss. That is a lesson I always instil in Aiknath. Look how happy he is.' She pointed to the happy couple. I looked at Aiknath. He was sitting with his hands clasped between his knees while his wife was carrying on a very energetic conversation with another well-dressed woman.

'He have me to thank for everything that happen now,' she said.

Roop had seemed withdrawn that day. He was walking around as if making a mental note of everything. I called out to him. As he approached, I saw that he still had that apologetic, shuffling walk, like if his feet were too heavy. His hair was now completely grey and the oil applied to the scalp was running down the side of his head, mingling with the perspiration. He produced a handkerchief. I told him about the girl I was getting married to. He was nodding his head in an uncomprehending manner. I sent my younger brother for a picture to show to him.

He looked at the picture for what seemed to be a long time. Then he said, 'You make a good choice. She is very slim.'

'We met at the university,' I explained.

Then he said suddenly, as if he had this to say and wanted to do so quickly, before he changed his mind. 'I have a little wedding present for you. Something that I talk to you about when you was a little boy. Is like if I had this present for a long time and I would open it bit by bit and show it to you, but now you getting to see the entire present.' He walked to his car and returned with a red, dusty notebook which he handed to me.

I read:

```
   I was travelling in a taxi to San Fernando.
The driver was huge and muscular. There was
another passenger in the back seat. The
driver never spoke during the journey. He
was whistling a song that reminded me of
death. While I was listening to this song,
I looked through the windows. Something is
wrong, I thought. There are no houses and
no cars. But there were many roads. We
passed a huge overflowing river. At this
point the other passenger just disappeared.
Then the driver stopped the car. Turning
around, he grabbed my throat with his
powerful arms. Looking at him straight in
the eyes, I told him, 'Unhand me, you
dacoit.' The hand slowly loosened from
around my neck.
```

I turned to another page:

```
   I feel sometimes, that I have a strange
power over animals. I first realised this
```

as a little child when all the neighbours'
puppies and stray cats came to our house.
My mother would quarrel and threaten to
poison them. Sometimes she would beat me and
make me stand in the corner with a concrete
brick on my head. After, I would look to see
if my head had grown any flatter. It did not.
But the animals kept on coming. They would
look straight into my eyes and then leave.
Later, there was this huge, ferocious bull
that had escaped and was threatening
everybody in the village. I went straight
towards the uncontrollable beast. My mother
tried to hold me back but I brushed off her
hand. Neighbours entreated me then they
looked at my eyes and the crowd parted
before me. A hush descended and the air
itself became still. The animal had sensed
my coming and it lowered its head. And then
it met my eyes. Years later everybody would
talk about this. People from afar would come
to visit me. As my fame spread, legends
grew. No one could explain how, as the
animal's eyes met mine, its body just fell
to the ground. As if in a deep trance.

'I interested in hypnotism these days,' he said.

Then he took the book, flicking through the pages. Look. Read this. Is one of my favourite.'

I took the book and read:

Life is like a ball of string stretched out
before us. We must unravel it carefully and
disentangle the little knots and kinks. At
the end of our lives we must be able to look
back and smile with glory and grandeur. The
sun must shine on our forehead, and, bathing
us with its radiance for all the world to

see. We must strive towards this sort of
ideal and then bask in the afterglow of
praise and adoration. It is only then that
we will be immune to the little microbes
that are constantly eyeing our privates.

I returned the book to him.

'Just some thoughts,' he said. 'Thoughts that come to me in moments of peace.'

Two years after my marriage his wife died of a heart failure and he successfully published two hard-cover editions of his book, 'Random Thoughts and Musings'. All the reviews that he received were favourable, although a letter written to the editor of a newspaper had complained that there were not enough illustrations in the book. But everyone else seemed happy.

In the days that followed he was invited to deliver addresses at weddings, christenings and school graduations. I remember reading an article in a newspaper about an address made at the inauguration of The Metaphysical Society of Trinidad and Tobago, of which he was the Founder and President. The article ended with a statement attributed to him.

'Success cannot be measured in quantita-
tive terms, nor can categories of human
beings. Similarly, in the eyes of the
Almighty, there are no Indian rogues or
Negro thieves, no white animals or black
robbers, no thin scoundrels or fat, powerful, wretched parasites. When we realise
this, we become free. My power does not stem
from any physical strength but from these
humble insights. I will, in my future books,
try to develop these thoughts.'

DIRTY RIVER

How can I say it? For me, who lived for fifteen years in a derelict, shambling town at its edge, Dirty River was a name of affection, not disdain.

As children we would go to the bridge and carefully climb down the wooden railing and begin to collect the perfume bottles, the multi-coloured cans, the discarded edges of furniture that had travelled for perhaps twenty miles, a present from the city. That was where our grandparents went to find work and from where they would return with parcels of clothing and cheap books, or sometimes, broken and empty-handed, going quickly to their beds, afraid of looking at us, of seeing our trust in them betrayed.

I always felt sad when grandfather returned that way, sensing both his guilt and his shame. When I dropped out of school to work in the cane fields, I often wondered if I too, years from now, would avoid my grandchildren's eyes.

When I went to the city beyond Dirty River these thoughts stayed with me. They were with me through the various jobs that I did: cutting the lawns of the wealthy lawyers in Roscoe Street, buying my first broken-down lawnmower and then my second and third. They stayed when I hired my two cousins from the village.

Speaking to Mr Roche that evening, studying the little twitches at the corner of his mouth, I realised he was afraid of me. For what? What had I said? I'd merely told him then that I'd grown tired of this lawn-mowing business. That I'd saved enough money to leave the countryside, that I was thinking of opening a small hardware or grocery store.

The next morning, I remember steering the lawnmower efficiently through the hibiscus, avoiding the concrete balusters at the edge of the lawn, cutting a clear edge through the flowers. He was there on the porch, looking at me through the smoke of his pipe. I was sweating and trembling, yet unwilling to turn off the engine, feeling the power of the machine flowing through me.

It overpowered me. I, with my muddy tall-top boots, standing at the edge of the ornate door mat; he, reading his newspaper, unwilling to acknowledge my presence.

I looked at the smoke curling upwards, intertwining with a potted fern. I knew he was annoyed; on the lawn the engine was still running. The words had formed in my mind: It is my machine. I can do with it whatever I please. I can't say if he had sensed this defiance. He carefully folded the newspaper and placed it on the table, next to the ashtray. He still avoided looking at me.

'The work is over. The lawn is cut.'

He was startled. I remember that. It may have been the firmness of my tone or perhaps because I had not spoken in broken English. He looked at me then, but when he spoke his eyes were on the lawn.

'Yes. It cut. I see that!'

Coming from him, these words seemed amusing, as if he was attempting some joke. But his face was serious.

'It cut nice-nice. Real nice-nice.'

Perhaps it was at this moment I sensed his intent, and I

remember that brief moment of weakness when I wondered whether I should leave.

'You is a born grass-cutter; nobody could take that away from you.' I felt the old shame hovering around, just beyond me.

'Everybody talented in they own way. The shop-keeper son will become a shop-keeper and the lawyer son will become a lawyer. Because that in they blood. Nobody could take that from them!' He was knocking his pipe on the ashtray. 'Everybody should know what they cut out for. That is the important thing.'

The pipe banged against the ashtray. The noise of the lawn-mower seemed remote, unfamiliar and powerless.

'You know I is a lawyer? You know what a lawyer does?'

I remembered reading about him in the newspaper; of writing to my family and explaining how I was working for one of the best known lawyers in the island.

At that point I wavered in my defiance. I stepped away from the rug.

Then he said slowly, as if a thought had just occurred to him. 'You see, by all rights, my son should be a lawyer now.' He drew deeply on his pipe, attempting to coax the tobacco to life. When he spoke he sounded breathless; suddenly old and tired. 'But you know what? He chose something else .... a dancer. That is what he wants to be. A dancer. Dancer.' He sighed.

I felt that I should leave then, but waited for some sign. He seemed to have forgotten me.

'You know what they say dancers do? You ever see them walk or talk? Look. Go back and cut your grass.' He seemed angry, as if I, in some way, was responsible.

'Too much change for a damn little island.'

I next saw him about ten years later. By that time I was already an established pharmaceutical salesman, transporting in my van, bandages, syringes and multi-coloured tablets to the various clinics and hospitals in the island. This may sound a bit immodest, but I had worked tirelessly at my profession and I was at that time not only a trusted and reliable salesman, but also reasonably wealthy.

Although at first I had resisted the idea — its absurdity in our climate — I found that the proper apparel, the wearing of a jacket, a tie and a starched, white shirt, gave me the proper image for this type of work.

It was much more difficult to change my manner of speaking. I remember with how much dismay and mortification — yes, mortification, it was not easy — I practised away my sing-song, lilting, native manner of speech. I read the grammar books and looked uncomprehendingly at the verbs, the pronouns, the conjugations. Finding nothing else so inexpensive, I bought all these strange comics with super-heroes flying and leaping from building to building. It was through these that I studied their language and tried to understand precisely how these Americans spoke. But it paid off. It has given me the edge.

I remember how impressed Mr. Rodriguez, the Director of Health in the County was when I wrote explaining why I needed my sales route expanded. He was surprised by the devious deeds of the other salesman (whom I had quite rightly called a dastardly misfit) as well as by the qualities I had promised to uphold: truth, justice and so on. The route was expanded and the hospital officials seemed almost to be looking forward to my arrival and delivery of drugs.

'Hi Sammy,' they would call out, trying their best to imitate my American accent. Then they would laugh.

I became the resourceful and frenetic salesman that we often see on the television programmes. In my case, not placing my foot on the doorway, but always thinking of something, always planning my next sale.

But that was then. Now I have no need for this talkative, cheerful business. As I said before, I am now a wealthy and accomplished salesman and even though the white shirt and tie have remained, the Americanisms have shifted to a more formal respectability.

It would seem as though I am moving away from my story but I have to explain this in order to capture that moment when I saw my former employer, Mr. Roche.

I had just finished my deliveries at one of the smaller clinics and was awaiting an itemised statement from the clerk. I have to admit I was a bit impatient that day. The clerk was in no big hurry; she was biting her nails and I could see tiny droplets of spittle at the corners of her mouth. This infuriated me.

'Listen. Am I going to get my statement or are you going to continue chewing your damn cud all day?'

She turned away with a batch of papers, leaving me with my anger.

Then I saw him. At first I was unsure. He had changed, and the years, they were not kind to him. The pink skin had become mottled. The square jaw had acquired a pair of jowls, like on an aged bulldog. The tired eyes were looking at the walking stick he held.

I considered.

The secretary had not returned. She was still in the office. I wondered at that precise moment whether he would recognise me. I doubted that he would. I had worked for him for less than a year.

Somehow, he seemed to realise that I was staring at him. And, as old people often do, his gaze very slowly shifted from his walking stick. Nothing sudden, almost as if he was just continuing some personal appraisal. I went over to the bench on which he was sitting. I could not find anything to say. Then he said,

'Sonny Boy, I saw you just delivering the medicine.' I nodded. He motioned with his aged hand. I sat down next to him. 'That is a good thing. Now I could collect my share and go home.'

'Where you live?' I asked.

'Where?' Then he laughed, starting with a dry, wheezy sound and ending with a splutter. He wiped his mouth with the back of his palm. 'As if you didn't know.'

So he had recognised me.

'Look, Sonny Boy. Look. Take one look at me and you would know.' He drew closer and I remember smelling his breath and finding the intimacy disconcerting. He took his thumb and pulled down his lower lip, allowing me to see the almost toothless gum. I was surprised and shifted away slightly.

'Is only one place you could find teeth like this.' He laughed his laugh again. 'Up in St. Clair. The Home for the Aged.'

'But what about your business, your children?'

'What business? What children? I have no one.'

I thought then of telling him but decided to listen a bit more.

'My only friend and constant companion is the insulin. You bring any?'

So, he was a diabetic. I felt a bit of sympathy then but more so curiosity. I wanted to complete the picture, to discover what had brought him to this state of dereliction.

'You bring any insulin.' This time it was not a question. His voice was muffled, almost like if he was speaking to himself. His eyes travelled downwards, looking at the end of the walking stick against the floor, examining the cigarette butts and the crumpled bits of paper. 'You know I used to be a lawyer. One of the best in the island. Wasn't a case I couldn't handle. All these cane-farmers and cocoa-growers used to bring their problems to me. I could have made millions. But I didn't make anything. No, Sonny Boy, that wasn't my luck. You see, when he died... on the very day that he died, I stopped charging people. They used to come and ask for advice and I used to tell them then to go along and not bother with money, that it have no value. I was no humanitarian because sometimes I used to chase them from the office shouting, 'Get out, all you low-class mongrels. Get out and carry all your money'. I used to tell them that sometimes. And I never, never charge a cent again. But people thought I was mad and they stopped coming and the business close. No more case, no more money, no more friend. You want to know why I telling you all this eh?' He did not explain.

He looked at me then, through his faint, mildewed eyes.

'You know... this face of yours look familiar. You use to be a cane-farmer at any time?'

'No,' I replied quickly, 'but my father and grandfather were.' After a while I said, 'I used to cut lawns.'

He had nodded his head, smiling, as if considering some private joke.

'Yes... yes. A lawn-cutter. You know, I had a boy who use to cut the lawn for me too. But that was years ago and he was a troublesome little fella. He would wait until I ready to read the newspapers in the morning and then start the engine, always circling and coming by the chair where I was reading.'

I remember looking at the brown, soiled clothing and the perspiration running down the sides of his face, down towards the neck and wondering whether I should tell him that this was not true.

'I recall the little scamp very well. Whenever I plant a new row of flowers, my beautiful little lilies and marigolds and chrysanthemums, he would pass with his machine and snip the leaves and cut off the little buds. I use to watch above the papers and see him smiling his cynical, little country-boy smile, as if he had repaid me for some distant, ancestral calumny.'

He was crazy. I felt no need then to explain; I just wanted to hear him speak about those wild illusions.

'And you know what the little rascal tell me one day? Listen carefully, cause I am sure you wouldn't believe. He said that he wanted to live in my house and take over my work.'

Yes. He really was crazy. I was sure that I had never told him that. I know that the thought had crossed my mind once or twice as I had seen him sipping his tea in the delicate, little china cups. But that was just a child's fantasy.

'He thought that I was unaware, that I never realise what was going on. But I knew everything. Even when he poisoned the dog.'

The dog! I almost exclaimed.

'The scratches on the car The grease on the walls... all of that I observe and I didn't say a word. He thought he was smart but I was smarter. If I had said one word, uttered one syllable, then he would have won his dirty little battle... Even when he wrote on the step: "My father is a pig".' The hands came together. He rested his walking-stick against his leg. 'So you realise what was really taking place, eh Sonny Boy? He was a crafty, crafty lawn-boy. All the time he wanted me to think it was Michael who was doing all these bitter acts. Michael was my only son.'

So Michael was his name; I hadn't even known that. I had seen him just a few times and had not, as I recall, ever spoken to him. It would have been an act of extreme audacity if I had attempted a conversation at that time.

'Now Michael is gone and that little lawn-boy is somewhere spoiling people's flowers and creating all kinds of country-people mischief.'

He placed his hands on his knees as if he was about to sit up. Then he said, 'But the strange thing is that I always admire that little boy. When I saw Michael coming and going with all of his idiotic, useless friends, I used to tell him to watch that little lawn-boy. But he never had time to listen to me. Going and coming. Coming and going. That was the only time I ever saw him. Morons! All of them. They couldn't ever begin to understand that little boy. And you know where he came out from? Perhaps you might remember that there was a place called Dirty River. I passed through there once or twice and I could remember the canefields and the broken down little houses standing on some long posts. The posts were long because every year the place used to flood and all the little vagabonds used to come out from their little, square houses and swim in the trenches and muddy drains. Brown on brown, and who could tell the difference. Now they don't call it Dirty River anymore. This bright, miraculous, government of ours calling it Riverside Garden. Riverside Garden! Such utter rubbish. Why they didn't call it Dirty River Garden instead. The houses get more rectangular, the drains get bigger but the place still flooding and I sure that all the little village boys still bathing in the dirty drains and open cess-pits. I used to think that it have too much change in this damn, stupid island but now I realise that nothing ever change.'

A thin, surly-looking nurse came just then and said that there was no insulin. She advised those who were affected by this news to return in two days' time.

'You see what I mean? Nothing will ever change. All the change taking place in our mind. We are propelled by promises and then broken down by these same promises. Nothing is ever forthcoming. Now I have to make this trip back to St Clair for nothing. Ah well.'

I told him then that I was going in that direction and offered to give him a lift.

In the van he remained silent, looking at the dirty roadside, at the garbage spewed in little unsightly heaps. We passed the fancy houses of the past plantation owners, and the newer, split-level buildings, not hiding behind foliage or flowers like the old houses, but thrusting out their affluence, inviting observation and envy.

Then we approached The Home for the Aged, which was itself once an old plantation house. But I saw how much of its original beauty had been denied. The windows had been removed and sections of the roof lay at the foot of a plastic pipe which served as a conduit for the sewage-disposal system. Strips of hardboard had been nailed all over the rotting boards and where the windows had been. I had to drive carefully to avoid the piles of rubble which were scattered all over the yard.

'My mansion,' he said as he dismounted, 'waiting to receive its aged emperor.'

I observed him leaning heavily on his walking stick, slowly making his way to the door and realised then that he had not thanked me for the lift.

'Mister. Get that van out from there. You think this is the White House you admiring?' It was a workman stooping behind a pile of boulders, heaping them on a wheel-barrow. I had not noticed him before.

As I reversed the vehicle I said, 'Listen chum, why you don't move out all this stone and gravel from this yard and plant a nice lawn?' In the rear-view mirror I saw the workman standing upright, looking either at the van or at the back of my head.

Now I have a little confession to make. That day, in the clinic, when he had asked about the insulin, I had known that there wasn't any. I recall Mr Rodriguez in the office, rubbing his wrists, gesticulating with his short, fat hands.

'What they expect me to do, Sammy. What they really expect me to do? They say they have no money to buy drugs and yet they drawing up plans to build all kinds of fancy hospitals with swimming pool and earthquake-proof building and all kind of fancy kidney machine. Sometimes I does really envy you, boy. Sammy, you don't know how easy your work is.'

Looking back now, I feel that it was because of this that I decided to pull some strings and secure a few bottles of the stuff. I knew, you see, that when he returned they would tell him to come back in two days' time. Why then, hadn't I told him? Because, I think, I really wanted him to continue recalling his story. In a way he was responsible for much of my success. That was something I had never thought of before.

I hesitate to use the word 'friend', but after securing and bringing the insulin to the Home for the Aged, he had become less distrustful. At first he was curious. He wanted to know if this was a recent service that was being offered by the Government. I had told him that it was.

'Then I better make use of it before it cut off', he said. 'Nothing of utility ever last very long. Do you know that there was a time when everything was free or just cost a few cents? When trains were on time, when offices were opened promptly, when even policemen were polite and respectful. But that was long ago, maybe before you were born. Then, I was young and I, together with some of my friends, would go to the Kingsley Club and there we would dance until the wee hours of the morning. The women, then, knew how to dress. I would go every weekend with a friend name Thomas. During the war he went to England and never returned. But it was he who introduced me to Angelique. She was so pretty. Even now I can remember her face. Her hands used to be soft and frail and her face was so pale that I wondered whether she ever went out in the sun. Let me show you something.' He returned with an old, faded photograph.

'That's her,' he said.

She was about nineteen or twenty when the photograph was taken. She was sitting on the ground and embracing her upraised left knee with clasped fingers. The face looked sad, as if she had lost something and the eyes were looking at some object beyond her feet but not captured by the photographer.

'Look at the hair tied in a nice knot over the neck,' he said, 'and the index finger; pointing upwards like if she is pondering some intimate problem.'

'Or reliving some experience,' I said.

'Yes.' He looked at the photograph for a long time. I heard a clicking sound and realised that his tongue was playing with his toothless gum, swishing around furtively.

'I should have married her instead.'

That night, on the bed, I told my son about how easy and pleasurable life had been in the old days.

'I thought you said it was hard work all the time.' His little eyes looked angry.

'Yes, but if you could see the pictures of how nice the girls use to dress up. With pretty frilly clothes and always looking at something on the ground.'

He ran out of the room shouting, 'Mummy! Daddy talking stupidness again.'

On my bed I felt I could hear the stifled laughter and the music filtering out from the Kingsley Club.

In the morning I gave a stern lecture to the boy who was packing the boxes of medicine into the van. 'Good grief! Can't you be careful with that stuff? You want to throw the goddam thing all over the place?' As I looked at his sullen, angry face, I realised with some surprise that I had momentarily reverted into the television salesman. 'I was just pretending,' I told him guiltily. I saw confusion replacing the anger. 'You is a hardworking boy,' I said uselessly and sped off.

We were seated on a concrete bench under an old soursop tree. The workman was very delicately unloading his wheelbarrow, afraid that the stones would crumble. But sometimes he would glance at us. A few days ago, as I was leaving, he had told me. 'I see you does be coming here often and I just want to remind you that sometimes people does talk without knowing anything. Maintaining a lawn is not something easy you know.'

'I know,' I had replied, increasing his confusion and then his anger.

Mr Roche — funny how I had stopped thinking of him by his name — was telling me about his early days as a lawyer's clerk, before he had gone to England to become a lawyer. At that point I realised that, since that day in the clinic, he had never mentioned Michael nor spoken of his marriage and his rise to prominence as a lawyer. The only time he had every alluded to his recent years was when he had mentioned that a few of his former legal colleagues had attempted to loan him some money. That was just after he had sold his house in order to repay the debts accrued over the years. He refused; opting instead for the security of the Home for the Aged. I wondered why he should want to punish himself. This, I could not understand at the time.

But he would speak of his youthful days with so much feeling, of the time when roads were well paved and buildings were sturdy and beautiful and when there was no corruption among government officials. He would recall the balls, the luncheon invitations and the social gatherings. 'Everything was governed by a clear code of propriety and everyone operated according to their social status. Look at the way things are now. Just a set of crab in a barrel and all of a sudden one crab just appear with a jacket and tie and telling everybody that he is not a crab any more. Ridiculous little place with ridiculous little people.' His voice trailed off.

Once he had startled me by saying, 'Without us, all of you would not have been worth anything of consequence, you know, Sonny Boy'. I hurried away, feeling sympathy for him, then anger.

That weekend, with both of us seated on the bench, and the workman casting curious glances at us, he was speaking with relish of an excursion to one of the popular beaches on the north of the island. I could hear his tongue swishing around in his mouth, trying to locate some bit of the past and I felt that I had to leave. But I knew that he was not boasting: he truly believed that the present held no place for him.

I was listening to his story but my eyes were on the workman, who had taken off his boots and was examining one of his toes. He was wriggling his toe and bending downwards, looking at the underside of his foot. Every now and again he would look at us.

While the workman was wriggling his toe, I had told Mr Roche that I wouldn't be able to bring the insulin any longer. He was surprised. Maybe I should have allowed time to finish his account. The old eyes looked at me with confusion and then a kind of angry shameful look. And then all of that receded. Perhaps he was somewhere journeying in the past and had already forgotten me.

Then he said, almost affectionately, 'It's all right, Sonny Boy. I know. It couldn't last. You go along.' For some strange reason I thought of his son, Michael, then.

I never saw him after that. The last time I heard of him was about a year ago when he was given a national award for community service. I heard the news in my office, just when the office boy, Fernandes, was delivering some xeroxed papers that I had requested. 'I wonder why him,' I had said aloud.

Fernandes had replied. 'They dust them out of retirement every few years.'

'But why him?' I repeated.

Well sir, is to maintain the correct blend,' he had replied, with a short, tight, acid look.

At about 4:30 p.m. last Saturday, I was in my garden, pulling out some weeds. I was thinking about how well-kept and beautiful this backyard garden was, and yet hardly anyone knew of its presence. My son was looking at the boy who came on weekends to work in the garden. The boy was removing some manure from a bucket and mixing it with dolomitic limestone. He wiped the sweat from his forehead on his forearm.

'Okay boss. Everything done for today.'

'Come for a minute.'

He was surprised. He looked at my son playing with the shears.

I told him, 'I just want to tell you that from next week I want you to start planting. I will do the mixing.'

'I didn't mix it good today?'

'Yes, but I want you to start arranging the garden for me. You will have to decide where to plant everything.'

'I was thinking about leaving,' he said apologetically, 'but the little boy getting big. Just now he will be able to help you.'

'So where you going?'

'Some place in town. Selling something. I didn't really decide yet.'

'You have any experience?'

'No. But I have to start some-way.'

'You will do good.'

He seemed genuinely happy. 'You really think so?'

'Well. You never complain or anything.'

'Sometimes I...'

'But you never...' I insisted.

'I could stay on for a extra week, if you want.'

'No - no. You make up your mind already.'

Washing his hands with the hose, he asked, 'You have any advice?'

I considered. 'No. Nothing I could think of.'

He looked hurt. He turned off the hose. 'Well, okay, then. I have to go now.'

As he was leaving I told him, 'Okay, hurry up. It was getting dark now'

He said, 'I accustom to that. Is like that always, sometimes.'

I collected my gardening implements and, together with my son, walked up the steps.

Mr Roche died soon after. According to reports in the newspaper; he was given a very elaborate funeral. I thought at first that it might have been partially sponsored by the state and in keeping with the national award he had recently been given, but then I considered whether the government might have been making a more political point: communicating to the public the demise of someone who was representative of a former period in the island's history and the way of life associated with that period. It was a neat, delicate way of emphasizing that such times were over.

Later on, I wondered whether the funeral had not, in fact, been organised by some of Mr Roche's old friends, members of the Kingsley Club and the Country Club with whom in his younger days, he had danced and feted away the nights in their exclusive, ordered environment.

The burial, I heard, took place in Paradise Graveyard, old, forsaken, overgrown with grass and bushes, the concrete flaking away from the once clean and ornate statues.

THE MINISTER OF ANCILLARY UNITS

Everybody hates me. But I can say with unequivocal assurance that this was not always so. There was a time when they would come traipsing to my door, never removing their dirty shoes, smearing mud all over the carpet, so spotless and immaculate before. And for what? To complain about some standpipe that was defective or about some road that had been eroded.

I shudder with disgust when I think of those times. How I hated ... no, loathed and abhorred this intimate way they possessed, as if I was some family member. Resting their garden-soiled hands on my shoulder or offering me — who had never tasted any form of alcohol — a grimy cup, half-filled with rum.

How stupid and pliable I was, pretending never to take umbrage at their petty, mundane problems. I remember this wedding where I was forced to render an address and this corpulent beast of a woman coming to me and proffering her over-weight little infant. Expecting me to wheedle and gush over her gift! I could have flung that child on the ground right there but, as I said, I was in those days, a benignant and obliging person.

When I was voted into power, I knew the frivolous thoughts that occupied their minds. Forget the curses flung at me when

I passed in my car. Ignore that time when they tried to march to my residence (in those days, I regret to say, I was still living in the outskirts of the city — a dangerous, unprotected place). These were minor occurrences; they really wanted me to once more prostrate myself to the barely controlled spite that resonated so vibrantly in their pithy minds. They hated anyone who tried to elevate himself from that morass of ignorance and would have been only too happy to see me stumble, lurching into the mediocrity that was so much their hallmark

But I was above and beyond all of this. I refused to allow myself to be besmirched by the taunts or by the upraised hands. I had finally broken away and would allow no one to disturb my progress. No one!

The night of the election results, about thirty or forty of my constituents had come to my home, beating drums, drinking and refusing to leave. When I emerged, they hung a garland around my neck and a few of the women kissed me on the cheek. But I was not angry because the situation demanded this sort of behaviour. I even made a speech, thanking each and every one for the work they had done in getting me elected. And perhaps that is where the trouble began. For days afterwards they would besiege me, beseeching, imploring and then becoming sullen and snarling with their primitive rage. How easy it is for these people to speak of ingratitude. In their eyes, I was some sort of sacrificial idiot, voted into power to do their bidding and to live out the rest of my life as an exalted slave. I do not state this with any sort of doubt. I am convinced! Why else would the pliant, lowered eyes explode with so much virulence when they are thwarted. As if the solicitous expression is merely a sheath for the real creature: the parasite within.

Let me relate an incident to demonstrate the level of cunning — or greed couched in desperation — as I remarked to a colleague the other day. It was a few months after the elections and I had only recently set up a constituency office. They had come — about ten of them — with their over-oiled hair slicked back, the white, or in some instances crimson shirts buttoned at the cuffs, and the inevitable rubber slippers, so incongruous and absurd. I must have smiled at that. One of them, obviously the leader, came forward with his mock humility. I can recall every word, every gesture.

'Well boss, you looking nice-nice in this new office.' He had waited for some returned compliment.

You looking so important that I feel proud that we have such a man like you to represent we.' The rest of the group had murmured their assent, nodding their heads. And that is why I feel you will understand we problem.'

There was the usual tirade relating to oppression, discrimination and racism. How they had worked so hard! And with no rewards, no thanks, no money, no anything. On and on he went.

I had to interrupt. 'But everyone works hard. You are not special.' It gave me a secret joy to observe the consternation on his face. Obviously expecting to forge a link through a common race and then seeing his tenuous premise so easily demolished. 'Why should you think that we alone have problems or that I should constrain myself to solving your particular woes?'

They were all speechless. The leader stood before me with his lowered head and then he said, 'Thanks boss. Thanks very much.' I saw his eyes blinking quickly, becoming red and then welling up with tears. But was I fooled? Was I ensnared with these people's obvious penchant for drama? Obviously not! I believe I am a very perceptive individual and here I am not speaking about my myriad research papers or my degrees and diplomas. I am speaking about the keen intuition that I possessed even as a child. I have long suspected that the envy and dislike that I inspired as a schoolboy must have stemmed from the realisation that I was not to be trifled with. Because they all knew, you see, that I could see beneath all the hypocrisies and crafted games.

On a day of boiling heat I had consented to cut the ribbon to indicate that a bridge had been repaired. Everyone had applauded but someone kept on clapping, refusing to stop. I saw him then. The leader of the delegation, with a twisted smile on his face. As I scrutinised the crowd with more deliberation, I recognised a few of his cohorts: those who had accompanied him to my office. I prepared myself.

One by one they flung their dirty insults.

'Why all you invite him here? You not afraid that he dirty up he pretty shoes?'

'Somebody take a picture quick. This is the last anybody go see him here for a long long time.'

'Look at him. Like a peacock with all he fancy clothes.'

I was hurried away but not before I heard someone say, 'You sure is the same person we elect or is a impostor? Look how different he looking and talking and walking. And look how he combing he hair. Somebody call the police fast!'

Why can't these people appreciate any form of perfection? As I state this though, I know it is impossible for them. If you observe them carefully, you will realise that they are either too fat or too thin. Either overweight or undernourished. They are never of perfect proportion. Perhaps — and this is a theory that I would, but for my innumerable tasks, have liked to develop — perhaps this physiological deficiency is a result of maladjusted thoughts and warped desires. Who can say that after centuries of adhering to a febrile philosophical system and harbouring all these negative feelings, there would not be some palpable symptoms. And yet they are so venomous when someone attempts any kind of improvement.

Look at me for instance. I am not so arrogant as to believe that even I do not possess my little problems. But I try. My chin, which can be described as receding, I now thrust forward so as to give it more prominence and a bulkier look. I wear my glasses low down on the bridge of my nose to restrain my nostrils which are slightly wide. Because I cannot really state that I am tall or slim, I try to walk as erect as possible with my tummy tucked in, allowing the contours to be immersed within my specially tailored clothing. As a schoolboy I had always found this habit of theirs, fondling their distended abdomens with so much devotion, to be extremely repugnant. Even as my own girth increased, I would never feel the pride that they felt, never succumb to the stupid attitude that this was a sign of wealth or of being well-fed.

Yet this, in my own situation, could have been avoided if it was not for my arthritis. I suppose I must thank my ancestors for that also! But how well I can remember the painful bouts in the gymnasium, the agony of hoisting the barbells, the diets and eating schedules that were so unsuited to my metabolism. But as you must have realised by now, this, instead of deterring me, rather acted as an impetus, spurring on my diverse energies into another direction.

What a life I am forced to live! Sometimes I feel that societies such as ours can never offer any solace to anyone with a heightened perception or with an advanced sensibility. They try to fit you into these narrow compartments from which you can never escape. Complaining has now become a national pasttime. And when they are not whining they are busy trying to pluck some ephemeral achievement from the distant past and attempting to fashion it into something of glory and pride.

Simpering on and on about the first civilisation on earth or about some abstruse, ancient, scientific discovery. And I, as an exemplar, am forced to listen to all the self-congratulations, without uttering a sound. However, I protest in other fashions, using different techniques.

I was invited to this seminar where the participants were scheduled to deliver papers dealing with the contributions made by the different ethnic groups.

When I saw him walking to the podium, I prepared myself. I was not fooled by his smiling, harmless expression, nor was I surprised at the sudden change of manner when he stood before the microphone. I have studied the schizophrenia of these people and I can predict every changing nuance and every shift in mood. They compartmentalise their emotions, locking and unlocking the doors as they see fit.

Try to understand his speech and if you can, assess the mood that would sprout so much useless rage. 'Today we are under siege because those we have chosen as our representatives have betrayed us. We sought change but little did we realise that the people we have chosen possessed their own hidden agenda.'

'Hidden agenda'! Observe the dramatic turn of the phrase, and understand how they couch their desires in the language of subterfuge and chicanery.

He had continued. 'Today I come before you, not to stir up any antagonism or to create any hostility among our peoples. But as I look at the contributions that we have made and at the long hours under the sun and at the thrift that formed so much a part of our lives, I am really confused as to why we are so often shunted off to small corners and why our legitimate demands provoke so much uneasiness. I don't know if anyone in the audience can tell me why it is that when one group speaks of ancestral heritage it is viewed as a legitimate search for their identity and their collective selfhood, and yet, when other groups just broach the issue, looking back at their own heritage, it is viewed with so much dismay and mistrust. I can never understand the insecurities that exist among our people. Why can't we be more harmonious and understand each other instead of just peering out from the periphery?

I did not leave then. I wanted to see how far the duplicity would extend. And I was not disappointed.

'A greater effort must be made to understand the diverse strands of culture that bind us together as a nation, for when there is a lack of understanding there is distrust. We must allocate an equal understanding to each religion, each festival and each culture.'

Eventually the defective anger came. 'Today I ask you to tell me whose fault it is if we have been cast adrift. As I ask you this question, I will propose an answer. In this audience there are a few individuals who are supposed to be our representatives, not only in a political fashion but also in the sense that they are the custodians of all our hopes and aspirations. And yet, I am disappointed to say, in both cases, they have failed us miserably. Do you know how many of them are ashamed of themselves and would, if it was possible, distance themselves from you? I want you, the audience today, to understand the self-contempt that exists among our leaders. But I call for forgiveness, for when they despise you it is their own weaknesses that they are despising. And when they pretend to be irritated by your demands, it is their own insecurities they are irritated by. Do not be very angry with them when you find that they are unable to fulfil simple functions, for they have never been and will never be the repository of real power. Do not be fooled when they preen themselves and parade before you, basking in whatever small adoration they could parasitize, because the moment that they stop their hypocritical behaviour, they will be devoid of true power. They know the true source of their power and have shaped their entire personalities, perhaps their souls, in order to accommodate this perception of theirs. They are forced to deny a part of their existence and life cannot be too easy for them.'

I had walked off then. Leaving, and seeing the heads turning, bobbing unintelligently from side to side, I could not help but notice how much they looked like puppets, lifeless and so easy to regulate. Just before I left, one of these puppets, bespectacled and nodding with false solemnity said, 'Those who cannot face the truth seek to fashion it to their own liking.' Behind me the morons all tittered.

This is the sort of thing I am forced to put up with. But I do not want to create the impression that it is always like this for there are times when I am in the company of more cultured and intelligent individuals and I know that my gifts have not been totally wasted.

I remember the cocktail party hosted at the residence of the French Ambassador. The President and his wife were there, as well as most of the magistrates, lawyers and prominent businessmen. I was speaking, for a great part of the afternoon, to the wife of the chargé d'affaires, a very demure and exquisite woman, if I ever saw one. Although I speak only a bit of French, she was well versed in the English language and I found her accent to be both enchanting and exotic. I know too, from the way she listened, nodding her dainty head, smiling every now and again, that she was equally captivated by my point of view. My modesty permits me to ascribe the point of view and nothing else (although I am happy I wore my fashionable three-piece that day).

'What an alluring island you live in.' How quaint was her

pronunciation of the word 'alluring'. I looked at her with deep respect.

'Well, as a people we still have our little primitive habits and rituals, but I am sure that by associating with the right international clientele we will soon iron out these little kinks.'

She smiled that demure smile. 'There are so many different er... cultures and such a profusion of colour.'

'Well, as you know; we have the best carnival on the planet. You must visit the streets at that time.'

'Oh, but the dust. It affects me rather badly.'

'Ah yes. I know what you mean. I remember how often I have to run inside to seek escape.'

She had looked at me with surprise, no doubt struck by my sensitive constitution.

'The beaches .... They are so beautiful though.'

I almost grasped her hands, wanting so much to convey my total agreement. But I resisted, not sure about the niceties of French etiquette. 'They are among the best in the world. I can say this without any doubts whatsoever. The only little problem is the sun.... and permit me a little confession, but I am partial to a sun-screening cream with an S.P.F. of about twenty. If I can offer you some advice, though, use the water-resistant creams. They are guaranteed to withstand anything the sea has to offer.'

I remember smiling to myself as I spoke to her, knowing how surprised she must have been at my knowledge of such delicate matters. Someone had approached just then and she had drifted off, no doubt to ponder upon what I had just told her. I saw her later on, among a small group, casting little glances at me. I know that I had to speak to her again. But whenever I approached she would drift away, attempting to create some semblance of indifference. But I knew.

'Pardon me, but when we spoke of the beaches and carnival, I forgot to mention something of equal importance.' Her back was facing me. Turning around, she seemed startled by my aggression, surprised that I did not use the subtle, circuitous approach. 'I am speaking, of course, about the mansion owned by our foremost plantation owner, Count Bouderle. Everything is just as he left it, even the trees, where it is rumoured he hung his slaves.'

'Very ...er.... fascinating.'

'Oh it is. It is. It is more than fascinating. Think of how the slaves worked tirelessly to build that mansion, carrying up the huge stones over that steep hill and then as a reward, were hung on that tree. What a droll sense of humour the Count must have had.' I laughed, my teeth glimmering.

She had moved away slightly, perhaps attempting to appraise me from afar, but I could not allow this, so I moved a step towards her.

'Perhaps you do not believe me, but there are many historical sights on this island. We've had such a varied history. Conquered by the British, then the Spanish, then the French and so on. And each group imparted something extra to us. So that you can find the English fortitude mingled with the Spanish liberalism and spiced with the French *haute couture*. The French have, in my humble view, given us the most.' Looking straight into her eyes, I told her: "Even now they are pledging us these special gifts.'

I know the direction you are expecting this account to lead into, but unfortunately that moment of such promise was shattered. Someone was saying loudly, 'Imperialism of any kind is dehumanising.' Knowing what to expect, I tried to draw her into a corner, giving her whatever protection that I could.

He was obviously in a state of inebriation and was unconcerned about the spectacle that he was making of himself. I knew him from the old days when we had campaigned together during the elections and even during that time he was an inveterate trouble-maker. Fortunately he did not recognise me and as he was led away, I heard him saying: 'We don't own anything anymore.'

Her eyes were wide and staring. I felt that perhaps she possessed some morbid curiosity about the drunk. I tried to explain. 'Unfortunately, we are saddled with people of that ilk. I cannot say why he was invited.'

'I would like to meet him,' she said.

'But why?' I asked with some amazement, even though the answer was already forming in my head. I told her tenderly, 'Please do not let this boorish behaviour detract from what has been a splendid evening.' I had added a touch of diplomacy then, saying, 'Let me assure you that no one can find any fault with this affair or with yourself.'

'But...'

'Oh. Don't explain. Let us occupy our minds with more pleasant thoughts. We were speaking about the Count, if I remember correctly. I gave a small reassuring smile then, and I saw her shudder noticeably; a small thrill of pleasure perhaps, coursing through her body. I decided to press home my advantage. 'I would like to offer my humble services whenever you may desire them. I can tell you that you can find no better guide. We will skirt around the noisy, troublesome towns and engage ourselves wholly in the delights of our past colonial connoisseurs.'

But sometimes I forget myself and allow the alluring part of me to take the reins. Seeing her there before me and observing her enchanting game — holding out until the last moment — I had forgotten the *chargé d'affaires*. Perhaps the feigned anger was meant for the surreptitious onlookers or perhaps it was contrived just that I might find her more irresistible. Such feminine wiles!

I did not see her for the rest of the evening but I could feel her eyes, moist and enticing, feeding upon me.

I have never been married and this has not been because of an absence of proposals. Sometimes at night, on the bed, I go through the newspaper and come across some photograph of myself and I imagine some of the things the mothers would be saying to their daughters. I look at the youngish face with a dignified smattering of grey around the temples and I imagine them planning, concocting their schemes and pushing their daughters forward, offering encouragement and advice. As I am relating this I can remember an incident that took place about a year ago.

The Permanent Secretary in my office, normally an incorrigible and intractable woman, suddenly became very friendly and accommodating. But I noticed a pattern to this amicability, for her little chit chats would always end in praises of her niece who, it was said, was a distant admirer and so on. Eventually an invitation was forced upon me and I, not wanting to offend, decided to visit their niece.

She lived with her mother and sisters in a huge, old-fashioned type of house a few miles away from the city. Journeying to that place and peering through the tinted windows of the car, I felt these twinges of panic. It was as if I was returning to an area that I had always associated with malice and shame, but not wanting to disappoint this expectant niece I journeyed on.

She was not at home when I arrived, so I spoke to her mother, a charming woman who looked as though she might be in her late thirties but who was obviously about forty-five or more. (If I had to hazard a guess I would say that she was exactly forty-seven). Well preserved, I thought to myself, observing the quick smile, the still smooth skin, the coloured hair neatly curled and sprayed. She had spent a great deal of time speaking about her sons-in-law: doctors, contractors and so on. After a while she had become silent and knowing what was required of me, I spoke of how I had completely restructured my ministry and of the great demands placed upon me. But as I talked I could see the admiration seeping out. I do not state this in jest; I really saw the admiration oozing out, being secreted from every part of her until I knew that I should stop. There was no need though, because fortunately at that moment, her daughter, the chosen one, arrived.

She possessed all the beauty of her mother, but with the tangy saltiness of youth. Observe the poetic inclinations when I am dealing with a beautiful woman — "the tangy saltiness of youth!" But to return to mother and daughter.

She dropped her bag on the sofa and hurried to the washroom. The mother, in that charming but firm voice, said, 'What happen, Natasha? You didn't see the Minister sitting here?'

'Yes I saw him,' she said, looking at me quickly and then moving away athletically in her tight-fitting clothes.

'These children,' the mother said. 'They so busy.'

'Who can blame them,' I said. 'Life is so short and there are so many things we have to accomplish.'

It was just a simple statement: something which comes to me naturally but I could see the simple profundity of what I had just said registering on her face.

'You know, Minister...'

'Yes?' I encouraged her.

'Maybe you too smart for Natasha.'

Ah, the perplexities of life. What was she imputing? A doomed marriage based on an intellectual chasm? Just an arbitrary but honest compliment? Or something more? I knew that I had to leave them. Hurry away before I was drawn into some amorphous web of febrile passion.

The dictates of my job permit very little time for frivolity now, but I cannot complain because I derive great joy in doing my work. I like to consider myself a workaholic. All the sacrifices are made in the national interest, and because I know there is no one else who would impart so much dedication and enthusiasm to do the job. It is with a great deal of satisfaction that I recall the Prime Minister explaining that my Ministry was designed especially for me, taking into consideration my special talents. And so the Ministry of Ancillary Units was envisaged and created.

It is not easy work, I can tell you. Sometimes these purveyors of inquietude, the members from the opposition bench, possess the gall to ask about the specific functions of my Ministry. I am not easily ruffled, but at such times I am not disinclined to unleashing the sharp edge of my eloquence upon these rabble-rousers. Imagine, one of them had the temerity to suggest that I was the Prime Minister's lackey. What a tongue-lashing he got that day!

It is the same old story. Envy stalks me like a crazed beast and, even though I am normally inured to such base emotions, I cannot restrain myself when they cast their apathetic aspersions upon either myself or my Prime Minister.

I can never forget the day when one of them called me a pothound, saying that my non-existent tail was continually devising new ways of secreting itself between my legs. I told him then that I preferred the position of a Government pothound to that of an Opposition mongrel. They all laughed uproariously, attempting belatedly to assuage their embarrassment.

This is why I am happy sometimes to be away from all this churlishness.

Like the time when I acted for five months as the Ambassador to Canada. Putting all modesty aside, I can say that I made quite an impact in the Canadian diplomatic circles as well as on the society in general. They were astounded to see someone from a small country operating as I did, asking for no favours and allocating blame without prejudice and, I dare say, without remorse.

The Canadians are not as cold and remote as they are made out to be in our little island and at no time was I ever treated badly. The troublesome ones were, of course, those who felt that I was some special emissary who would wave a magic wand and solve all the inevitable entanglements that they had gotten themselves into. It is amazing how these trouble-makers leave their country and retain this trouble-making capacity; as if it is some special benediction that they always carry with them.

Demand heaped upon demand. Always the irritating belief that they are entitled to this special treatment. I need not mention also, how easily they speak of ingratitude.

They would come to my office in droves, sometimes gathering outside the closed gate before the time of opening. Then they would stand before me (I had deliberately removed the chairs so as to reduce their interview time) and fidget, balancing on one foot and then the other, looking at my face for some sign of understanding. Invariably I would tell them that they were wholly responsible for their predicaments. Selling their houses or leaving their well-paying jobs, did they now expect to be ceremoniously greeted and garlanded, with employers in Canada fighting each other to hire them? I would study their dejection and look at their capricious eyes flickering one minute with irresolution and then narrowing the next with apprehension.

How weak these people are. How often they bring shame to me. Their ancestors springing from a distant and remote place where, if one were to flick through the pages of a history book, one would only encounter a long line of conquests. Defeats and degradation, and yet they boast about their pervasive, accommodating way of life, able to swallow up everything and everyone and yet survive. So when they boast about their ability to survive they are also boasting about their ability to endure defeats and shame. Everything is built around defeat. Observe the way they celebrate these defeats, removing the shame and stressing only the sacrifice they have borne; dramatising the consequences of their weaknesses. Nowhere have they displayed any steadfastness of purpose or gained any respect. Chased from area to area, afraid of fighting back, they fight among themselves. I cannot think of a more snivelling race of people.

They embarrass me, yet I am thankful that everyone can see that I am different. Sometimes I feel that I have spent my entire life trying to achieve this. Like parasites, they try to draw from my own reserves of strength but I will have none of that. That is why they are so incensed by me and why they are so wrathful about my achievements. Sometimes, in their desperation, they stoop to flattery; gushing with praises, which even if not totally untrue, are delivered for the wrong reasons.

Do not think me heartless when I say that there were some days when I longed for the nights so I would be able to pursue my unofficial duties or pay an unscheduled visit to an opera house or perhaps just while away the time in a quiet restaurant, soaking up the ambience and forgetting for a moment, the weak, languid faces I had observed during that day.

I have my life to live. While I am constrained, in an official sense, to listen to all the sullied hopes, I cannot let that impinge upon my own relaxation or appreciation of the finer things in life.

Away and apart from all these wretched aspirations and thwarted hopes, I am in my element.

Like when I was asked to deliver a speech about the threat of nuclear war, to a small university. How the power flows through me at such times! I am not content to just sermonise about abstract evils. I place the dangers at their very doorsteps. I grab the edge of the rostrum, I cradle the microphone, I lower my voice. I allow the barely restrained passion to flow from me straight to the audience.

Afterwards, members of the audience would approach me, offering their congratulations. But I can never respond adequately for I am, at that time, still trembling with passion and my mind is still suffused with pain and concern. It is only when I am safely cloistered within the security of my dimly lit penthouse, imbibing the haunting strains of a concerto or a sonata filtering out from the radio, that I allow myself to unwind, allow the tension to dissipate.

Can they ever understand this? What must I do to show these people that I am occupied by far more important issues? If only they could peek into the inner realm of my mind and observe its nobility of intention, they would see how irrelevant their problems are.

One evening, while lying on my sofa, and after a day of intense frustration, I concocted this encounter based partially on several real incidents. (Yes. My imagination can also move in that direction.)

Allow yourself to smile when you grasp the absurdity which I am trying to demonstrate.

In this incident I am seated before my desk and my hands are resting on its shining, smooth surface. Someone enters saying, 'I am in trouble. I need help.'

'What kind of trouble?' I ask, smiling.

'I want a job.'

I lean back. 'A job. I see. And what kind of job would you desire? A corporate planner? A manager?'

He answers, 'Any kind of job will do.'

I summon my secretary and dictate a letter. He gets the job. The next day he returns. 'I didn't like the job.'

'Why?' I ask him.

'It don't suit me.'

I arrange something else.

He returns.

'What is the problem now?'

'I don't like this kind of work.'

I become curious. 'Would you like to do my work?'

'Yes.'

So I offer my job to him. He comes back after one week, his face haggard and drawn.

'You can have back your job.'

'Why?' I ask calmly.

He hesitates. 'Too much work. I thought it would be easy.'

I refuse. 'It is yours now. I cannot do anything.'

His face contorts with fear. 'No. No. Please. I beg you.'

'Too late,' I say.

He produces a gun from his pocket. 'I knew you would say that.' He fires, the bullet passing through his throat. I summon the secretary.

'Take this body away from here and please see that this rug is cleaned.'

Race. Racial suspicions! Racial fears! Racial jealousies! When I returned from Canada that was all I ever heard. They would organise meetings and invite me. I never turned up. They would send letters stating their puerile experiences. I never replied. And then I was appointed as the chairman of the committee to probe all these fears and insecurities. I was told by my colleagues that I should be very tactful since to alienate any section of the community would be to relinquish a large part of our normally reliable voters. For days and nights I pondered, wondering what I should do. Since I was constrained by the suggestions of my colleagues, I could not act in the manner I would have liked to, scuttling their preposterous notions and abolishing all their unrealistic desires. And then it dawned on me.

In my report I recommended that we should not restrict ourselves to the present situation but should also examine aspects of the plurality that existed during the pre-Columbus period. I suggested that we should look at the relationship that existed between Caribs and the Arawaks who, as the original inhabitants of the island, were more important than any other grouping. We should dissect and analyse, I stated, every aspect of their relationship and try to determine how they perceived each other.

Need I state how much hatred this report engendered? But they could not protest because I had drawn legitimate conclusions and prioritised the appropriate historical antecedents. Perhaps they began to realise then that I was a man of untarnished principles and that I would never breach these principles. I might even add that I had forced a kind of respect for myself upon them.

All of this was evidently responsible for the incident that occurred about a month after the report was published in the press.

He was formerly the mayor of the Southern Borough. Now he was a proprietor and the head of a co-operative that exported agricultural items: vegetables, flowers and so on. He was well-known and involved in various charitable organisations. 'I want to congratulate you,' he had said.

At first I was wary. 'We all have our contributions to make. As you did years ago.'

'My time has passed and now it is up to people like you,' he said.

I resisted a smile. 'I just do my job.'

'I know that. And I know also how hard it must be for you.'

The smile came then. 'Difficult? Sometimes I feel that I thrive on these difficulties, especially when I think of how boring life would be otherwise.'

'It take a good mind to think like this.'

'All my life I was prepared for this sort of thing.'

After a while he said to me, 'But you don't feel any regret?'

'Regret!' I almost laughed. 'Regret is for fools. And in any case, why should I feel regret?'

'Because not everybody might like you.'

'Who cares? They never liked me then. They don't like me now. Perhaps they will never like me.'

'I like the way you talk about the Caribs and Arawaks.'

'The first people,' I said.

'They gone now.'

'Except in the pages of the history book.'

'They was good people. My favourite tribes.'

'They had their day,' I told him.

'And now we have ours. That is why I come to you. I want to be your campaign manager for the next election'.

'But that is more than a year from now.'

'We have to start early.'

'Why me?' I had asked bluntly.

'Because I see you is somebody who don't care about what people think. In plenty way I could understand the way you does think and feel especially when you see your own people turn against you.'

'Like Cassius, they crave too much.'

'Ha-Ha. Exactly.'

'They feel they could purchase me with their contrived hurt.'

'Never happen!'

'And what of the so-called leaders, the pious uplifters of men,' I sneered. 'They have done nothing of substance for the country. They seek refuge behind their little constituencies and never dare to establish a wider realm.'

'Exactly.'

'I am the first, the only one who has risen to such a position of prominence. Compared to me they are just insignificant nondescripts.' Warming now, I told him, 'I can say that I am the only one who has broken away from all this racial stereotyping, the only one to cross the barrier. Do you see how the other races, by contrast, all respect and admire me?'

'They know you is not bias.'

'And respect my integrity. I often get these letters of congratulations.'

'Except that fella from the papers, Mr. Matthews.'

'He is an anachronism. He is too steeped in the past to understand the demands of the future.'

'Mr. Minister...'

'Yes...'

'You have this way with words.'

'It is another of these gifts. That is why I am driven forward. Not for praises or adulation but because I feel that I have been chosen for something special.'

'All of them before you was just jokers. Too bias.'

'I feel that I am ushering in a new age of politics. Those who complain now will come to me with bowed heads and ask for forgiveness.'

'Especially when you become the Prime Minister.'

I observed him and saw the honesty, the simplicity and the devotion. I got up and placed a hand on his shoulder.

'Do you know something?'

'Mr. Minister?'

'I think we can work together.'

When he came a few days afterwards he told me, 'I read in the newspaper that you will be flying out to Switzerland in a few days' time.'

'My work is not confined to this island.'

'Don't hold back when you reach in Switzerland. Let them see the kind of man you really is.'

'How can I hide it?'

He giggled softly. 'And before I leave, let me thank you, on behalf of the co-operative, for all the assistance. The subsidies will really help.'

I dismissed him with a perfunctory wave of the hand. In my mind, I had just disembarked from the plane and the United Nations representative was waiting to greet me.

As he was leaving he said, 'While you across there don't worry too much because I will be working hard in my capacity as your campaign manager.'

They still hate me, but it doesn't matter anymore. Their malice cannot reach me any longer and I have become immune to all the spiteful anger.

In Switzerland, all the international journalists had queued up after my initial contribution. I had spoken of the need for immediate multilateral disarmament by the super powers — my pet topic these days, and I had given vent to all the innermost qualms that I had harboured all these years. They had listened attentively when I spoke of nuclear war, nodded when I gave a historical analysis of European tension, of the long Franco-German rivalry, of the period preceding the first world war of English isolation, and marvelling, no doubt, at my intimate knowledge of their history. I explained that they should not be deceived by this brief lull in tensions, since, in the past, this had merely served as a prelude to terrible hostilities and wars. I cautioned them that societies in a state of flux were liable to

THE MINISTER OF ANCILLARY UNITS

prove the most unstable and dangerous: former enemies creating alliances which were unthought of just a few months ago. And they had applauded spontaneously when I stated that I was prepared to become a symbol of nuclear disarmament even if I had to prostrate myself at the feet of presidents and kings, commoners and criminals, anyone in fact, who would listen.

Even though a British tabloid referred to me as 'The Radioactive Man', the other respected journals and magazines were rapturous about my delivery. One of them stated, 'The third world has finally found a voice'. My tributes are too numerous for me to mention, but in my living room in my Geneva mansion, I have framed some of them, as well as pictures of myself appearing on magazine covers. A few chosen friends would look around and smile wistfully, realising that factors other than ego operate within me.

Perhaps one day I will return. My campaign manager is still hard at work. Just the other day he wrote, stating that he had always wanted to work in the United Nations, but for now, I am firmly ensconced in my work, meeting with heads of state and expressing my disapprobation of the proliferating arms race.

I am not an easy man to please. I state my case with a resonant voice and a firmness of tone that allow them to see exactly who they are up against.

At last. People can see me for what I really am. At last, I am free.

CLOUDS

That night Cheryl could not sleep and she twisted on the pillow making small, complaining sounds. The mother patted the girl's frail back a few times, her fingers running along the protruding spine and caressing the soft hair that fell along the back of her neck.

She groaned silently when she heard the inevitable request for a story.

Half-asleep, she told a story of a little girl who had been captured by a dragon and left in a cave. It was only when she felt the anxious, heavy breath beneath her palm that she realised that her imagination, inkling towards sleep, had suddenly become perverse and that her story was frightening the child. This had happened before. Sometimes she would awaken and see Cheryl sitting up in bed, saying, 'Mummy, I don't like this kind of story. Let the dragon die in the end, not the little girl.'

Then, in a voice holding neither anger nor affection but twisting towards both, she would say, 'Okay Cherry, time to sleep.'

She never know how long her daughter would lie awake because she herself always fell asleep first.

When she awoke the next day, Cheryl was already up and in the kitchen. She heard tins rolling on the table and the stool

being dragged across the floor towards the refrigerator. She yawned, stretched, and placed one foot on the floor. Cheryl, hearing the creaking on the bed, came running into the room.
'Surprise, surprise!'
'Surprise?'
'Yes, come in the kitchen and see.'
'In a little while.'
'Now,' she prodded. 'Come now.'
She went into the kitchen and saw the bulging bag. She unzipped it and saw the biscuits and the soft drinks, the mutilated sandwiches and, beneath all of these, the towels, hairbrushes and swimming costumes.
'All of this?'
The pert little mouth crinkled into a smile.
'Look like I have nothing to do again.'
'Everything my own self.'
'Okay, give me a minute to shower.'
'But hurry. The beach will fill up just now.'

Cheryl heard the water falling and dragged the bag to the garage. Then she sat on the steps and waited. She tried not to think of what she had dreamt that night. Of the water drying up and leaving miles and miles of hot desert sand sprinkled with dead fish and crabs and dying turtles. In the dream, the sand felt like fire.

In the car she looked out for the coconut trees, knowing that they were a sure indicator that the beach was not too far off. They passed houses, the bigger concrete structures closed securely, the smaller wooden ones with the windows and doors open and women with curlered-hair peeping out, or sometimes children scooting outside and running in circles in the yard, playing among the water-barrels or between the little clumps of allamanda and crotons. As the car slowed around the bends, sickly-looking puppies yapped and chased at the tyres, causing her to bolt into the middle of the seat, eyeing the door nervously to make sure that it was locked. Past the Baileys Bridge, where young men holding out bundles of crabs stepped a few paces into the road shouting, 'Lady, buy these crabs for the huzzie', and, as the car sped by, saying angrily, 'Arright, the next lady go buy it for him.'

Cheryl saw the coconut trees and tugged excitedly at her mother's blouse.

But she was elsewhere. She was thinking about her new job as a secretary in the County Council, about the other, younger women there who had offered her only a wary coolness, as if each was afraid of being displaced from the chatting groups. But she was not interested in displacing anyone; she was not even sure that she wanted to be a part of their giggling gossip.

There were times however, when the loneliness and the strained glances pained.

Age brought so many insecurities, she thought, forcing someone like her to withdraw even more into a forlorn remoteness. Once she would have been able to not only deflect the hostility, but also to insist by her own defiant aloofness, that hers was the stronger, the more potent emotion. She marvelled that she could have once been the repository of such naked confidence.

Cheryl saw the houses appearing nearer to the road, the shops closed, the boys perched on the bridge railings. And the coconut trees. She could already feel the wet sand beneath her feet, the water swirling up around her ankles. Her excitement grew. She would look for the round, black sea-balls and throw them into the water; watching the waves bring them back to the shore. A thought came to her. 'Mummy, can we dig for chip-chips and carry them back home with us?'

Yes,' she replied, feeling the familiar wariness descend. She passed her hand over her forehead, fingering the curl that fell like a closed circle.

Someone at the office had said, 'Look how she always fixing that stupid piece of hair. And always peeping in that little mirror.' They were right. Always looking for reassurance in the mirror and returning with a depression that she could not quite understand. Sometimes, in the middle of typing some memoranda, she would instinctively reach for the mirror, pat her curl and then continue typing. A messenger, dropping some parcels had said, loud enough for her to hear; 'Just now the whole damn thing will fall out, the way she does be wringing it, wringing it, all the time.' But the curl was not the focus of all her attention; sometimes she would glance at the lines forming under her eyes or at the sides of the mouth, the hardening of the skin, and the pores which seemed to grow larger with each passing day.

'The sea, the sea! We reach!' Cheryl began jumping up and down, her thin legs giving her the appearance of a panicky water bird. 'We will eat afterwards, okay?'

'Be careful,' she said, as she watched her daughter running awkwardly towards the waves, observing the moment of trepidation as the first ripple touched her feet, the involuntary shudder as she prepared to leap into the water, the excited smile when the tousled head emerged.

There were just the two of them on the beach that day. Beyond the waves, the sunlight bounced off the water and the green haze shimmered with a dangerous beauty. This was how it must have looked in the beginning, this daunting isolation, so forlorn and yet so darkly tempting. The sea had not always brought these thoughts to her. Once it had suggested freedom and release; now it pointed towards dissolution.

Cheryl sat on the sand, her knees bent, the soles of her feet placed against each other. Within the circle formed by her feet, she dug little holes, searching for chip-chip shells. Already her cheeks were beginning to redden from the sun, but she was happy. She watched the holes filling with water, and then the water seeping through the sand. She watched this process several times and then moved nearer to the shore because the tide was rising and the foam was swirling in little eddies around her legs.

The peninsula, covered in green, about five miles away, looked like the head of a huge dragon nestling in the water. She looked around for her mother and was relieved to see her sitting on a log that had been washed up by the sea.

Her mother had taken off her slippers and was tracing a pattern on the sand with her toe. A solitary coconut tree arched its way out of a clump, its curved top swaying over her head.

Cheryl looked up hurriedly but noticed that none of the nuts were dry. She did not want to think of anything bad happening to her mother. She saw a seagull swooping downwards and hurling itself towards the sea. She felt sorry for the fish it might have caught. Something felt prickly beneath her feet. It was a sea urchin, round and covered with sharp spines. She removed it from the sand, looking for eyes or a mouth or any other signs of life.

'Look, Mummy, a starfish. It still living 'cause the small sharpen things still moving when I put it in the water.'

For two months she had gone to church, vaguely seeking redemption, ever-lasting peace and other things she had always associated with religion. She found none of them, finding instead a cloying sense of guilt and irritation.

Perhaps she had made a mistake; she should have chosen one of the older, more established churches instead. She had never felt comfortable with the pastor's bristling spirituality. He was a chubby, energetic young man who was always gesticulating and pointing to members of the congregation. 'You there. Yes, you! I want you to take Go-hod in your heart this very instant. Come on, do it. Open up your heart and fe-heel him enter!'

At first she had been mildly amused by the range of emotions that flickered over his face, each seeming more contrived than the last, but later, she began to suspect that his anger was not unreal, that there was some barely restrained paranoia inside him that could be unleashed at any moment upon members of the congregation.

'Out Satan, out. Get out and leave this miserable sinner alone. Leave her for me. She is mi-hine now. Mi-hine!' She had this uncomfortable feeling that he was always referring to her. She looked carefully to see whether the pointing finger would linger accusingly in her direction.

She had persisted, though, for a few months, just for Cheryl, hoping against hope that some cure would be found.

Two boys, about thirteen or fourteen, came running along the beach, a black and white mongrel tailing them. Cheryl stood up, watching the dog carefully. They moved on. She looked at her mother and smiled with relief. Nothing should spoil this day. She concentrated once more on the sea. She heard the noise of the waves rumbling in the distance, the noise faint and indistinct, then more powerful like a truck faltering up a steep incline. The waves gathered momentum, bristling with urgency, the noise coming from everywhere all at once as they crashed on the sand just in front of her, before their life-force frittered away, hastening back for renewal in the ocean. She observed this process several times, focusing only on the sounds, closing her eyes, hearing the distant rumbling reaching a crescendo, coming closer to them and then melting away.

Crash!

She made an involuntary sound: a shriek caught in her throat and then, sensing that the danger had passed, relapsing into a subdued 'Oh.'

Another wave crashed by her feet. As she was about to move closer to the shore, she opened her eyes and saw the spent waves, drained and lifeless, the water lapping round her knobby knees, posing no threat. She felt suddenly invincible.

'Come! Come on!' she taunted the water

'Come and do your bestest.' She felt that the sea understood, she sensed the anger in the wave, this one bigger than all the others, gathering power, coming closer. She shut her eyes tightly, still saying defiantly, 'I not afraid of you. You can't do me anything. Not me or my mummy.'

And it came on, refusing to break, unwilling to lose its angry strength. Then it was upon her, buffeting and thrusting, surging around her waist. She strove for anchorage, her toes curled around the sand. The water subsided, she folded her arms, watched her mother and smiled. She felt the breeze blowing around her; lending her its strength. 'I win,' she said. 'I win. Nothing could ever harm me again!'

After the girl's father left for America, he had written only once, just a week after his arrival, telling her he had found an apartment and had made some new friends. He wrote of the difficulty of getting a suitable job and of his intention to look at the various hospitals in New York. That was the last she had ever heard of him and, although she was not really surprised, it sharpened her sense of betrayal and hurt. She drifted in and out of offices, gaining and losing employment, unwilling or unable to participate in the socialising taking place around her. She began to steel herself for the day when Cheryl would be stricken down and she would be alone once more. Her desire to be inviolable became obsessive; no one was allowed to enter her secret world of hurt and anger. And as Cheryl survived, refusing to let go of her enthusiasm for living, the mother lost her assurance, lost her fierce determination to be immune to every emotion save those concerned with her child. Now she wondered at the soothing certainty that she had previously felt, becoming uneasy at the notion that her daughter's illness had been an excuse for weakness and selfishness.

But was she really selfish? Hadn't she stayed with her all these years, looking after her, seeing her grow weaker and more dependant? So many times, people on the streets, in the pharmacy stopped to look at her child, offending her at first, and then giving her a pride which she feared had no real foundation.

She watched Cheryl, still and upright like a post, not flinching at the waves around her feet, her face thrust forward. This was the determination which had driven her crazy at home, a defiance that would spring from her eyes and tauten her limbs, a silent strength that would remain until the mother, not the daughter, had to relent. Now she thought: this was what was responsible for Cheryl being alive today, a stubbornness she had mistaken for some kind of retardation. Perhaps she should die like this, away from the trauma of hospitals and transfusions and ventilators.

She covered her face with her hands, trying to push away the thought.

Lying on the shore, her chin propped against her wrists, her eyes closed once more, Cheryl tried to smell the sea: the salty water, the fishes that she imagined were swimming a few feet away, the sand under her face, the wind bringing all these smells together just for her. She licked the droplets running down her lips, savouring the tangy, fishy saltiness. At school the other girls had laughed at her; they should see her now, not walking with jerky, little footsteps but just lying on the sand, comforted by the water caressing her belly.

'No game for she.'

'Let she play with the children from abc ketch-a-crab class.'

'Why she just standing up 'cross there, looking at we like that?'

'Leave she. Don't bother. Who want to hop-scotch first?'

Let them play their stupid games by themselves, she thought. I have my mummy and this beautiful sea, just for myself. But the recollection disturbed her. She rose and went into the comfort of the water, feeling the waves wash away the shame. She felt strengthened, renewed, at peace.

Then the sky grew suddenly dark, the blueness obscured by dark-grey clouds that seemed to be scurrying across it like small animals being pursued. She looked up and saw why. Another monstrous, dark animal was hot in pursuit, moving nearer and threatening to engulf everything in its path. She went further in, imagining the water bonding to her skin and forming an invisible armour that made her invincible. She felt the tingling in her legs as the water touched her body, forging its miraculous shield, and then the special feeling moved up to her waist and then to her chest as the water performed its magical task. She looked up anxiously; time was running out; the creature was almost upon the little animals. She became worried, frightened. Then she saw her mother was still on the shore, standing up, her hands covering her face, and she no longer felt afraid. She surged ahead, her eyes on the sky, her tiny hands flailing insistently against the waves. The ocean encircled her neck. Just a little bit more, she thought, straining against the water. And then just as the dark-grey specks were swallowed up, she felt the water rushing over her face, felt the hair streaming upwards. I am safe now she thought. Nothing could ever hurt me again.

THE METALWORK TECHNICIAN

The job of a metalwork technician at the oil refinery at Pointe-a-Pierre was not a very difficult one and Mr. Hoobnath Hingoo was adept at all the various tasks that he was called upon to perform — welding, soldering, joining, cutting pieces of steel. He was happy when he was bending over a lathe, his thin body vibrating in tune with the rhythm of the machine. But afterwards, in the canteen listening to the engineers speaking casually and confidently about their work, he would feel belittled and humiliated, almost as if those easy references to their jobs were aimed especially at him, slighting his honest labour.

Dislike, then envy and finally intense hatred came easily to him. He could not bear a recently hired engineer who was always speaking of how he could modernise the plant if he was given the opportunity. This young engineer, dressed casually, his long hair blowing about, his voice loud and assured, sent Mr. Hoobnath Hingoo spinning out of control.

He would listen to him in the canteen, speaking to the other young engineers about the projects he had done at the university. Hoobnath, hearing the precise technical terms being used, felt that this was aimed only at him, attempting to shunt him aside. He would listen to the laughter and observe the youthful, flippant faces gathered around the table and he would look at his own calloused hands.

It bothered him. Alone at home, he would think of his skill with the machines, knowing each of them so intimately, realising immediately that something was wrong if the deep, purring sound was interrupted by a minor clanking or if a pulley needed adjusting, or the motor needed some lubricating oil. He remembered a story that his Standard Four teacher had told the class. About men who were such perfect riders that legends had sprung up about the horses and the men being one creature. He would think then of his own body joined to a machine, both vibrating happily.

He could no longer draw comfort from these images. More and more, he felt trivialised by the young engineers. Sometimes he thought: just put them in the machine shop for one day. Give them a simple task. A piece of iron to drill some holes in. He would imagine a finger being suddenly separated, or the drill piercing a wrist, blood squirting all over the place. And the long-haired engineer. He would imagine some item of clothing being caught in the machinery and hear the screams ebbing away as the machine pulverised the flesh. And Hoobnath Hingoo would smile, tiny wrinkles forming in protest at this unexpected action.

The smile, however, would be premature. The next day, in the canteen, he would feel again the same helpless fury at the spontaneous chatter and laughter. There was no respectful moderation in their conversation, just an arrogant boisterousness which embraced everyone. Everyone but Hoobnath Hingoo, who remained alone at his table, casually stretching his long arms along the cross-bar at the top of the bench, trying to give the impression that he was perfectly at ease, or perhaps engrossed in solving some complicated problem that someone had brought to him.

But no one would notice and the hands on the bench would

begin to tap nervously and his face would droop, the features seeming to drop away from the face.

They feel they too bright and I too dotish. It should have a fire breaking out in the refinery one day. In their section. There would be a momentary satisfaction, the tapping on the bench would become less frenetic. *Barbecue the whole side of them. Grill them nice and black. Afterwards we could have a sale. Grill engineers. Going cheap. Eat as much as you like. We have plenty more stocks. Just say the word and we will grill a few more.*

'I got this offer to work in Alaska. Good money and everything but I not too sure yet.'

Yes. Go to Alaska. It too cold to have fire over there. It have these things call igloo. Go and live in a igloo. Certain parts of you body does freeze up and drop off.

'But I waiting on a reply from Texas. You know that once you in the oil industry over there, you business settle.'

Hoobnath considered his future. After working for almost ten years he might be promoted to a Technician II and then he would work for another ten-twenty years and, if he was not retrenched in the interim, he would then be retired and given a stupid, old watch. And the refinery newspaper, *The Tri-Star*, would have a picture of him receiving this watch and then there would be this little caption beneath the picture talking about twenty-five years of loyal and dedicated service. *Dedicated service! Not in Texas or Alaska but right here in this little fowl coop they call a refinery.*

'This place is really a dead-end. The plant itself too old and obsolete. Sooner or later they will have to sell out.'

Sell out! I better get me deed ready. Oh God, man. Oh God. Why me? Why is always me? Why I didn't go to university instead of that stupid trade school. Then nobody couldn't sell me. And I could come here and talk as loud as I could and everybody would just have to listen. And respect me. Not them little locho over there. Dressing and talking as if this is they father backyard.

Once he had come to work in acid-washed trousers — fashionable at the time — with innumerable flaps over the many pockets and at the waist. It had been a disaster.

'What happen Hoobnath? Like you liming in the distilling section again? You have to be careful with all them dangerous chemical, you know.' For the rest of that day he moved from machine to machine, vibrating at different levels of intensity, never looking up, his teeth clamped down.

Then his luck changed. The supervisor for his section was transferred and Hoobnath felt an immediate affinity with his replacement; not distant and aloof like his predecessor, but receptive to suggestions and willing to discuss them. Like Hoobnath, the supervisor felt that his ambitions had been thwarted and he realised that he had been given this supervisory work not because of his qualifications but rather, because he was about to retire in a few months.

They began taking lunch together in the canteen. Hoobnath felt at liberty to discuss his problems and frustrations. The supervisor would always lend a sympathetic ear; like Hoobnath, he was disgusted at the recent trend of replacing experienced workers with university graduates.

'Just theory,' Hoobnath would say 'No practice. That is why production falling so. One day one of them will end up in real trouble.' In moments of recklessness he would say, 'If I happen to meet the General Manager anytime, I will tell him that straight away.'

The supervisor would agree, 'That is the correct thing to do. The very correct thing.'

Every now and again someone would call out to the supervisor. Sometimes they would come and sit for a few minutes.

THE METALWORK TECHNICIAN

Hoobnath appreciated this, although he could become agitated if the visitor overstayed his welcome. He had staked his claim and considered the supervisor to be his possession. He had already begun to adopt some of the supervisor's mannerisms. 'That Thompson is a real scamp. Looking so innocent and yet his overalls always full up. You don't hear how it does be clanging any time he make a step? I don't trust him. I very well don't trust him,' or 'I don't understand how Singh does always be sleepy so on the job. Is the very said thing diabetics does do.'

That was how he dealt with anyone who appeared too friendly with the supervisor. One day, the supervisor said, 'The old Cooper is just the kind of worker to have. Any problem that need fixing, just call the old Cooper.'

Hoobnath listened.

The next day he told the supervisor, 'You don't see how the old Cooper does be carrying on? I not saying anything but I just watching him. One day the old Cooper will receive a nasty shock...' He stopped on that ominous note.

He soon discovered that he had a talent for these declamatory remarks. 'You see that long-hair engineer over there who always babbling like a woman and boasting about how bright he was in university? Well, I hear from a reliable source that he was a real dunce who get through the university because he father uses to pass the money. Is only because they had plenty money. Very plenty money. That and that alone save him.' The supervisor listened carefully, smiling cynically, and casting sidelong glances at the cluster of engineers.

'The very thing I suspected,' he said. 'The very said thing.'

Hoobnath began to relax, feeling freer than he had ever felt before. He discussed all of his blocked ambitions, stressing too his modest nature and the viciousness of his enemies (of whom, in his accounts, there were many). The supervisor absorbed all of this bitterness, occasionally spewing out some caustic observation, inviting Hoobnath to continue.

As Hoobnath became more confident, the scurrilous rumours that he had invented about those he hated became more libellous. The supervisor looked on approvingly. He told him, 'Just now will be elections to vote for the shop stewards. We need somebody very determined and very brave for our area... But who we will put?'

'You think that I might fit the bill?'

'The very said person that I had in mind.'

'But I not too popular...'

'Don't worry, I will talk to a few of the boys and tell them to vote for you.'

Hoobnath was elected with very little trouble. At the meetings he had spoken of information gathered from 'reliable sources' of plans to retrench workers, of plans to cut salaries of the technicians, of increases in travel allowances for the upper level management and finally of his opponent's close links with management.

'Is not up to me to say why, but some other people just going in and leaving other people office as if is they own bedroom. You have to be careful with these people. You have to be very careful. Watch the cars and see how new tyres appearing just so, and then ask where the money coming from.'

They mistook his propensity for *mauvais-langue* to be a kind of recklessness, something well-suited to this business.

He became more confident in the canteen, calling out to workers he barely knew, 'Paul! Come here. It have something very confidential that we have to discuss.'

He developed a new gruff manner of speaking, which was really a modification of the supervisor's cynical fashion. He would lower his normally high-pitched voice until it had acquired a grating raspiness, the voice coming from somewhere within the throat. 'Watch that Anderson fella carefully, eh. He up to no good. You see how he always walking sideways like a crab. Well don't trust him. The old Anderson up to no good.' The supervisor, sitting opposite, would clear his throat, making at the same time, little grunts of approval.

But Hoobnath's joy was not complete.

The group of engineers sitting nearby still ignored him. Occasionally though, when his voice became overly loud, one of them would look in his direction and mutter something. Then the entire group would break out laughing.

Once he had heard the word 'insecure' and he knew that they were talking about him. Trying to sound casual, he said, 'Some people does spend the whole day in the canteen as if they have nothing better to do.' Then in a lower voice he said to the supervisor, 'If they boss know how they does be carrying on, he will get damn vex for sure.' Almost as an afterthought, he asked quickly, 'You know him?'

The supervisor shook his head. 'But I know somebody who know somebody who know him.'

He persisted. 'Maybe if the boss get to know, they will change this rum-shop behaviour. Always laughing and talking stupidness and wasting time.' A sudden thought struck him. 'But if you think about it, maybe they not really wasting time, because sometimes I does hear them talking easy and shoo-shooing and looking round suspicious...' He whispered, 'Sedition. That is the very said thing that going on.'

The supervisor looked at the group. 'It wouldn't surprise me one bit.'

Hoobnath continued, 'From the very beginning I did suspect that. They can't fool me. I watching them very closely. Especially the long-hair one.' He felt comforted, and although he had no idea who or what they were plotting against, the very sound of the word strengthened him. 'Seditioners!' he said aloud, drawing a moment of confusion and then a fresh round of laughter.

That evening, after work, he went to the Princes Town branch of the Carnegie Library and asked the librarian, Mr. Bashir Ali, for information on industrial espionage. The librarian looked at him suspiciously. 'Check the encyclopaedias across there.'

But Hoobnath was disappointed. The entry had alluded only to large companies which were in competition with other large companies. The refinery that he worked in seemed too small and insignificant to possess any industrial spies. But he refused to completely dismantle his belief. He knew that the young engineers were up to no good. But what?

For the next few days he watched them carefully, not letting them know, though, that they were under such careful scrutiny.

It was useless. He could pinpoint nothing. The supervisor noticing his seething frustration, told him, 'I will be retiring in about two months time.' Hoobnath barely heard him. 'Since the first time I see you I feel that you was ambitious. I know that nothing could stop you. You always have the welfare of the plant at heart. You don't like stupidness. Even if you have to write letters.'

'Letters?'

The supervisor changed the subject.

Hoobnath smiled.

First of all, Hoobnath wrote a letter to the General Manager, Mr. Leighton Smith, detailing his suspicions. He awaited a reply during the course of the week. There was none. Next, he wrote a letter to the Chief Engineer, stating, more specifically, his disgust at the behaviour of the new engineers in the canteen. He also mentioned his information, derived from reliable sources, of the high incidence of drug-taking among recently graduated engineers. This time the letter received some attention. He heard the long-haired engineer saying. 'These senile old fellas have nothing better to do.' They all laughed but Hoobnath could sense that some of the exuberance was gone; he could sense their discomfort during the conversation.

He wrote other letters, castigating, impugning and implicating. His reliable source seemed to be everywhere. Then a sort of frenzy took over. He began saying in a very loud voice, 'The General Manager don't like what going on in this place at all. He very, very disturb.' Speaking with relish, he would say, 'He tell me that he might have to start firing from a side. Especially some wasteful people. He just can't take it anymore.' He was determined that the source of his power be exposed and he imagined with delight the fear that he was inducing. He pictured the young engineers saying with worried, panicky voices, 'We should have never got on the bad side of the old Hoobnath.' And the long-haired one saying, 'But how we could have ever guess that he had so much string to pull. I think we should apologise to him right now.' In his picture all of them would agree solemnly, their heads bowed, their minds numbed.

One Monday, after penning a particularly vicious letter and depositing it, unsigned as usual, into a mailbox, Hoobnath ambled across to the long bench in the canteen. The young engineers were already chatting. Hoobnath noted that the laughter was muted and that the voices were not as loud as usual.

'Prem!' His voice shot out across the canteen. Everyone looked up. 'Come. Come! I want to chat with you.' Prem, an apprentice technician, came and sat opposite Hoobnath.

'I not satisfied with the work you doing these days.'

Prem was confused.

Hoobnath continued. 'I find that you does always be liming on the job. We have too much of that in this place already.' The brows furrowed. 'You better watch yourself.'

Prem's confusion vaporised. 'I not doing me work? I liming too much? And who the hell is you to tell me this? A damn mule like you. You not happy with me? Well write out a list of me fault on a piece of paper and give me tomorrow and I will see what I could do.'

Although Hoobnath was unprepared for the sarcasm, he said, 'Okay. Is your funeral, not mine.' As Prem got up and was walking away, Hoobnath said, 'Somebody ask me for a report. I might just have to include certain people in this report. I could tell you that somebody mightn't be pleased at all.'

'Somebody could kiss my ass,' Prem said, still walking, not looking back. A ripple of laughter ran through the nearby tables but Hoobnath was not overly concerned; he was already formulating another letter.

He smiled. *We will see who will kiss who ass*. But his satisfaction was stillborn. He heard an engineer saying, 'Boy, you lucky. You damn lucky.'

Lucky? He felt the old weakness returning. The long-haired engineer had recently joined the group at the table. He had a letter in his hand and was excitedly waving it about.

'You mean you really get the job in Texas?'

In Texas. Oh God. Oh God.

'Let me see the letter,' a fat, cheerful-looking engineer said. 'Signed Mr Ernie Springer. Look like a friendly kinda guy?'

'Friendly kinda guy? Like you all reach up Texas already?' He fired a mock blow at the fat engineer.

They collapsed in laughter

Not now. Not when I have all the power.

'I suppose to go up next week and sign the contract.'

'It must be have plenty perks, boy?' another, very young, engineer asked.

'Well, yes. U.S. dollars, company house, citizenship in a few months, if I want it.'

'Company house? You alone in that big house across in Texas?'

'Not for long.'

'Aha! They will deport you for that,' the fat engineer broke out laughing.

'Deport one of their best engineers? You crazy?'

'Maybe you could pull a few strings,' the younger one said, half-earnestly.

'Yeah. Fix up for we across there.'

'Don't frighten about that. That will be the first thing that I do when I settle down.' He seemed serious. 'The whole bunch of we across there. Just imagine.'

Everybody escaping? Now? This can't happen. He felt like a furnace, the fury, like a fierce fire, raging out of control. If I could find out the company in Texas and the manager, I could warn them. But the contract almost sign already. And all this time I didn't even suspect anything. Just when I was getting ready for them.

'A friendly kinda guy! In a few months you will be talking just like that.'

'No ways. I will never give up this accent.'

'You wait and see.'

The long-haired engineer glanced at Hoobnath's table. He said, in a voice loud enough for Hoobnath to hear, 'Where the frog today? I only seeing the tadpole.'

The laughter felt like sharpened knives. He could bear it no longer. 'So I is a tadpole?' Suddenly he realised that there was nothing more to say. He got up slowly. 'So I is a tadpole? A little frog?' he repeated uselessly. He spun around and walked away.

That night he wrote a lengthy letter:

I am ashamed to be working in this environment. There is too much laziness and corruption. I have a long list of all the crimes that I make a note of over the last six months. Crimes that will make the General Manager feel very ashamed. And why must we hire all these useless engineers. They only wasting company time and money. It have so many good and experienced technicians who could do twice the amount of work in half the time. Everybody saying that we must progress, but I say, progress for progress sake is no progress, or even the opposite of progress.

He stopped there, realising that he could find nothing really damaging to write.

He could feel the engineers slipping away, could feel his own confidence waning. He felt weak with hatred; lost and helpless.

The next day, when the supervisor reminded him about the retirement function and indicated that he would like him to give the vote of thanks, the debilitating hatred was still with him. On the day of the function it was there, overpowering him. He heard his name being called. When he walked to the microphone, his hands were trembling. He searched for the prepared speech in his pocket. Even while writing the speech he had been in a haze and now he barely remembered what he had written. Reading with a shaky voice, he was surprised at the formation of the words, by the thoughts. After about twenty minutes, the chairman coughed, trying to catch his attention. Then he gesticulated angrily to the person in charge of the audio system. Members of the audience grew restless, then angry.

Afterwards, they commented. 'He feel he is the General Manager. Saying that he will fire as he see fit.'

'And talking for so damn long. I thought that it was suppose to be a vote of thanks.'

'It sound more like courthouse speech to me. Accusing everybody just so.'

'Must be on drugs.'

'Not drugs at all. I know him good. That is he normal way.'
'You shouldn't use the word "normal" in describing him.'
'A whole blasted hour. And instead of thanking, he criticising.'

But the supervisor did not seem affected.

'Hoobnath, I would like to thank you. Is the best speech I ever hear. The very best.'

Hoobnath seemed in another world.

'Don't take them on, son,' the supervisor said.

Son? Vaguely, he was touched.

'Don't take them on. I agree with everything you say. Okay son?'

He placed his hand on Hoobnath's shoulder.

In a little more than a month, Hoobnath was married to the supervisor's daughter, several years older than himself and possessing a plainness so normal and unredeeming that it seemed almost like a virtue.

Inevitably, he quarrelled with his wife, berating her for faults that she could not understand. He flew into terrible rages because of her manner of speaking — which she had inherited from her father. He would shout at her, 'So you is a damn, blasted Englishwoman eh? Old this, old that, old everything.' Sometimes his anger would be reduced to dry taunts. 'Oh, the *old* food didn't prepare yet. Like Princess Anne went horseback riding again. But don't worry, I will just drink some *old* water, it good for the *old* constipation.'

She began to spend weekends by her father, then entire weeks. He would tell her, 'Give him some room, he will change. I know the old Hoobnath.'

Later in the year, the old Hoobnath applied to the engineering faculty of the university and was turned down. The moments of rage came more often. One day, his father-in-law summoned him. Hoobnath arrived, sulking. The father-in-law was brief. 'I not so young again. I have just one daughter and all the retirement money wasting. Is something I thinking about for a very long time.'

His hands shook with pride when he hung the sign:

'HOOBNATHS MACHINE SHOP'. He looked at his wife. 'You think this will do or I should give a little more info. Like me experience and skill and all that. Eh?' He winked at her; she blushed. 'Maybe something like, "Come here for practical work, not theory",' he continued.

That night, his wife, feeling his body vibrating on the bed, suspected that their problems had ended.

THE FUNERAL

The taxi dropped him by the wharf, just past the crowded, cluttered depot where the blue and silver buses came careering out from the repair yard, stopping briefly to engage the waiting passengers: the old women, their baskets filled, returning to Sangre Grande, the school children throwing their bags through the window and then scrambling through the front entrance, the lower-ranking civil servant, ties hanging from shoulders, clutching their cheap briefcases, cursing their luck and everything else.

He walked up High Street, climbing the steps, holding the railing to steady himself, trying to conserve his energy, avoiding as best as he could the smell from drains and piles of garbage.

Waiting for the line of cars to come to a stop at an intersection, he told a startled policeman, 'If I had to wait here for one more minute, I would have jump straight in the middle of the road and let the Government pay for my funeral.'

He hurried past the pavement vendors displaying their stock of leather shoes and elaborate leather sandals. When one of the vendors said, 'Come and look at these nice shoes over here, old man,' he barely heard him.

Spying the bottles of sweet-sickly aromatic oil from a distance, he covered his nose. A young woman, coming from a store, plastic parcels under each arm, eyed him and frowned, clutching her parcels tighter. Worthless little thing, he said silently, imagining the contents of the parcel. When his mind encountered soft, diaphanous lingerie, he stopped. He curled his lip up further, staring at the other women. They looked away, quickening their steps.

Past the hospital now, rising like an aged monstrosity from among the newer rectangular buildings. Windows opened; a few heads peeped out.

As he was about to cross the road, a vendor asked, 'You want a doubles, partner?'

If a man spit hard enough from that window, he could spit straight in that open pan, he thought. 'I not in the mood for eating spit today.' The noise of the traffic drowned the sound of the vendor's curse.

He bought some bananas. He saw the boy, barely twelve, replacing the bunch. 'Who land you thief this from, boy?'

The boy looked guilty and confused. 'I grow it myself. I have no parents.'

'I have no parents, too. And look I not selling any bananas. I never sell any in my whole life. The thought exhilarated him. I am a self-made man. He dropped the skin into the cardboard box. Never thief anybody. He peeled away another banana skin. The first to own a left-hand drive. American. Eight cylinders. He savoured the banana, squelching noisily. Before they take away everything from me. The fruit seemed suddenly unripe and abrasive in his mouth. He spat it out in the cardboard box.

'Two dollars,' the boy said. He paid the two dollars.

He remembered the foolscap sheet in his pocket. 'Now, where that newspaper office?' he asked a boy with a mohawk hairstyle and an earring on his left ear. The boy seemed eager to help but his directions were confusing and contradictory.

He told the boy, 'Young man, I can't understand one word you say. The way you all dress nowadays, I not sure if is Indian or Creole, if is rich or poor, if is young or old.' The boy smiled sheepishly, not sure whether it was an insult or compliment. 'I not sure whether is male or female.'

The smile disappeared from the boy's face.

Then he spotted the aged building. With great difficulty he pushed open the door and entered.

'We not open yet,' a fat, surly woman with an assortment of multi-coloured bowclips and a face like an affronted pig, said.

'How you not open and I just walk in?' he said jovially.

'We not open till half-past one,' the woman said defiantly. 'I alone working on this shift.'

'But the sign outside say one.'

'I say I alone on this shift,' the woman said, raising her voice.

'And why the hell you didn't put that on the sign outside then?' He became angry. 'What you expect me to do for the next half an hour? Go outside and help the policeman direct traffic?'

'Look mister...' she saw the face, old but strong, the steady eyes, the barely controlled indignation. She said instead, 'You could sit down and wait. It have some papers across there. You could read if you want.'

He took one of the newspapers. He read aloud, 'Carpenter kills wife and children.' She peered at him from the little circular aperture in the glass window. 'Man throws acid on his mistress. Claims that his children have no biological right to call him daddy.' When she saw him looking at her and perhaps reading to her, she quickly resumed her filing and notations. Every now and then though, she would glance at him from the corners of her eyes, while he read aloud.

At quarter past one she told him, 'Okay. What is it you want? I ready now.'

He said, 'Wait until is half past one. I still have a few more things to read.'

But he did not read any more newspapers. He took out the foolscap sheet from his trousers pocket, opening the folded paper by flicking it through the air with a twist of his wrist, making a loud sound. The woman swivelled her chair away from him.

He read aloud. 'Rajmoonie Gosine passed away peacefully in her sleep, on the morning of Saturday 10th August, 1989. I wonder how they know that she passed away peacefully. Anybody wake her up just before she die and ask her if she was sleeping peacefully? Look, hand me a pencil.'

The woman frowned, rearranged a hair-clip but gave him the pencil.

'Scratch "Mother of five and grandmother of ten". Scratch "Cousin of so and so". Scratch "Sister-in-law of three". All right, give me another piece of paper now.'

The woman gave him a sheet. She was attempting to summon some anger but because she was unaccustomed to being spoken to in this manner, the vexation which was so normal to her did not come. How easy it would have been for her to lace her voice with sarcasm. She glanced again at the dishevelled shirt sticking out from his trousers, the uncombed hair, the rubber slippers. These country people, she thought. Let him open his mouth again.

'Office Lady!' She jumped. 'Listen to how this sound. "Rajmoonie Gosine died and will be cremated. Come one, come all". Everybody will be happy now and no one will be offended.'

She searched for anger but said instead, 'It sound unusual.'

'Unusual? What usual about death? You know that this woman who die was my wife? You find that was usual? You find that I look usual? Take this paper and file it and publish it for one week.'

She looked at the paper. 'But the cremation is tomorrow. What is the use of publishing it after that?'

'Publish it still,' he said 'I always wanted to be a publisher.'

On the way home, in a taxi, he told the driver, 'I just advertise my wife death in the newspaper.'

The driver shook his head sympathetically. 'So when is the funeral?'

'No funeral for her. She will get a cremation. Hindus believe that burning removes all attachments.'

The driver, still in a sympathetic voice, said, 'It must be hard for you now.'

'It not as hard as you think because I was preparing for this for a long time. We've been married for fifty-three years. At the age of eighteen. In those days I was just an ordinary farmer. A small scale farmer. Not like now.' The driver examined the old, crumpled clothing and concentrated on his driving.

The car emerged from the town, away from the crawling traffic, the pedestrians nonchalantly crossing the streets, the small stores with extravagant billboards, the larger stores with smaller, modern-looking Plexiglas signs, past the roundabout planted with yellow heliconias bestrewn by straggly weeds, the fire-brigade station, the derelict rumshop, the hardware with a sign stating: 'Recession Prices. Come and Check us Out'. And then the empty lots, the abandoned houses, the sugar-cane fields.

'This is where I work for almost twenty years. Loading the cane on the mules. In those days we had no tractors and harvesters and taskers. Everything was manual. That is why I so strong today. Grief mean nothing to me. How long you been driving this taxi?'

'Me?'

'Yes. I'm speaking to you. You see anybody else in the car?'

The driver did not like the stern, schoolteacher's tone but he said, 'For two years. Off and on.'

'What do you mean, off and on?'

'Sometimes when things tough, I just park it up.'

The driver heard the heavy, brusque, humourless laugh and began whistling the tune of a popular calypso.

For twenty years I work in this place, he thought. Twenty years! Things were always tough but I never give up. Twenty years of struggling and then that brief moment of financial security. Still, he had been able to send his children abroad to be educated. This is why he alone had to make all the arrangements. But even as he thought of this he knew it was not true. He had deferred the other tasks: going to the police station for the death certificate, arranging for the pitch-pine wood used as a pyre, negotiating with the funeral home; all of this was handled by his son-in-law. He wanted, however, to be seen as being in control, not burdened by grief and irrelevant despair. This was how he had lived his life and even though this attitude had created enemies out of many relatives and former friends, to him it was a sign of strength and steadfastness.

The taxi slowed to a stop. He paid and dismounted. 'Don't park up when things get tough. Let it always be a test for you.'

'Okay, uncle.' The driver, appearing relieved, sped off.

Deo climbed the hill where the abandoned vehicles lay, already covered over by vines and grass: reminder of a better time. He saw the two-storied concrete estate house — also abandoned, where he had once lived with his family.

About five years ago, at a time when just he and his wife remained, they had moved out of that house and had constructed, a short distance away, bit by bit, a small, wooden, one-bedroom house, devoid of windows, of plumbing and electricity.

When everyone had blamed him, saying prophetically that he was dragging his wife — who had loved the rows of ginger lilies and anthuriums, the mahogany-stained furniture, the marble face-basin — dragging her to her death, he had replied that he had passed the stage where the acquisition of material things was important. For the rest of his life, he told his friends, he would be a hermit.

He did not care for the sound of the word. It reminded him of crabs and of being cloistered, but the other associations, the ones derived from the religious texts, gave him a special mystic thrill. After a while, no one attempted to argue with him because he would give long, tortuous explanations of the different stages in an individual's life and of the ancient patterns that had to be obeyed. Some of his relatives suspected that the move from the comfortable estate house to the frugal, incomplete, wooden structure was really a means of accommodating his failure: the loss of the heavily mortgaged land to the bank, the purchasing of expensive agricultural equipment that proved useless because no one could operate it, the insistence on cultivating an unprofitable crop. Reeling from losses, year after year. And now the hermit's life, so well suited to his decaying business; turning financial failures into something romantic.

That night he awoke with a start, imagining that he had seen his wife above him, above the bed, a soft, injured look on her face.

In the morning, he went outside, smelling the dew, the early morning air, the cane flowers bending in the breeze. He walked bare-footed through the fields, the breeze pressing against his pajamas, his wiry chest and arms; the soft mud splaying his toes, covering his heels. He remembered that soon all his daughters and sons from Canada and England would be arriving and he went back in to the hut, lying on the bed, his muddy feet leaving brown smudges all along the bed sheet.

He must have fallen asleep like that because he was awakened by someone rocking his shoulders and shouting, 'Oh God, Dad! Don't tell me you gone too. First mother and now you. Don't do me this.' It was his second daughter, the only one of his children who had not migrated. Soon after the death, she had bustled about — her husband, a perpetually worried-looking man, in tow — visiting the funeral agency, complaining about the stiff, uncaring attitude of the employees, worrying about the quality of pitch-pine, the quality of camphor, the quality of ghee. Although she might have been offended by the letters she received from her sisters, detailing their metropolitan burdens: extra expenditure for the children attending ballet classes, swimming lessons and piano lessons, for the last few days she had been everywhere, offering advice here, offering consolation there, her husband behind her, supporting and admiring her grief. Eventually, the sisters were forgiven; she understood the tasks which only she could handle.

'If you continue rocking me like that, Radhica, then I might dead in truth.'

'How you could make joke at a time like this?' Radhica said, wiping her eyes and turning to her husband, attempting to coax some admiration from him to equal hers. He saw the sacrificial smile and understood.

'You have to be strong to do that,' Ramlakhan said uncertainly.

'Okay, Daddy. I have to go now and see about all the arrangements,' she said in a very tired voice. 'Ramlakhan, you stay here and console Daddy.' Ramlakhan looked trapped. He steeled himself for a philosophical lecture on life and death.

Ramlakhan was relieved when he heard, 'Come outside and breathe some fresh country air.' Together they walked out of the one-roomed house.

'Who put up the covering on the tent?'

'I organise it,' Ramlakhan said eagerly. 'With a few workmen. We try to work quietly so you wouldn't wake up. I know how tired you must be.'

'And how the tarpaulin have so much hole? Suppose rain start falling.'

Ramlakhan looked crestfallen. 'Was the only one we could get. I think mice do the damage.' He looked around furtively, searching for his wife but she was some distance away, speaking to a group of remote relatives who had arrived from Chaguanas or some distant area and who had come early in order to avoid the heavy traffic. A few cars were already streaming in. 'I better go and arrange some chairs,' Ramlakhan said desperately.

'You stay right here. Everything will arrange for itself. This is a funeral, not a wedding.' Ramlakhan resigned himself. 'Now tell me this. You make any arrangements for your own death?'

'My own death?' Ramlakhan was startled. He attempted a smile.

'Suppose you die tomorrow. What will happen to all the children?'

'It have insurance and the little bank account,' he fumbled. But Ramlakhan's fears were premature; the question was merely a preparation.

'That is why I not worried today. I sent all my children abroad to get educated and now all of them have good work. Except Radhica. I had to keep somebody reliable nearby.'

Ramlakhan acknowledged the compliment, smiling awkwardly.

'You understand how hard her job is? To take care of me. And you.'

Ramlakhan got up suddenly. 'That is not Uncle Seebaran

coming?' He referred to him in the fashion of his children; Uncle Seebaran was really a cousin of his wife. He was a tall, compact man and he seemed cheerful and amused. But that was not unnatural; he had deposited his wife within the group of women and she would convey all the grief and despair. The women in funerals were the specialist mourners, the men —unless it was a very close relative — were content to discuss random things: the state of the business, inquiries about long-forgotten relatives, the indiscretions of the government.

'What happen, Ramlakhan? How you not with Radhica?'

He, missing Uncle Seebaran's cheerful sarcasm, replied, 'I going now. I going now.'

'Ramlack man, you is a real joker,' he said, slapping him heartily on the shoulder. Then he turned his attention to the old man, sitting on a rented metal chair, his feet crossed, a cynical expression, faint and almost tolerant, on his face. 'What I will tell you, Deo? These things just happen. Is you alone now. All the old people pass away one by one.' Uncle Seebaran, despite being a nephew, was just a few years younger than Deo. The casual tone was derived from this rather than the family ties. 'You have to keep the old flame burning.'

Deo slapped his chest. 'This old man always keeping the flame burning. Next ten-twenty years when you go also, he alone will still have the flame burning.'

'A whole generation just pass away.'

'That is the law of nature and we must adapt to it. What else we will do?'

'You look good,' Uncle Seebaran said suddenly, tenderly.

'I have to look good. Just now Shobha and Vijay and Subhash and all the rest from Canada and England will come and it will be my job to console them. Wait and see. You will hear them from right down the hill, moaning and groaning.' He laughed, his lips slack.

At that very moment, Ramlakhan who had been sitting nearby, sulking, rose up excitedly, shouting, 'Look! Look! That is them. In the car coming up the hill.'

In the car, a well-dressed, middle-aged woman was explaining something to a boy of about seven years. The boy's head was out of the window and just above his head was her hand, pointing to the cane field and the abandoned vehicles, and wagging with energy, the fingers flicking here and there. The finger pointed towards Deo, then the hand withdrew into the car, now instructing the boy how he should behave. In the front seat, next to the driver, a thin, morose-looking man sat impassively, staring straight ahead. He produced a handkerchief, coughed into it and replaced it neatly in his shirt pocket. The car stopped. Radhica walked towards it, breathing heavily, careful not to hide her fatigue.

'Sister, look how we have to meet.' Sobbing now, she encircled her sister. And who is this big man here?' She cupped the boy's chin. 'The little swimmer,' she said sincerely, momentarily putting aside all the old feuds. Then she composed herself. 'Shobha, you go and see Daddy. Nobody know how he taking it. He smiling and talking now, but *I* know what taking place inside. *I* was with him all these years. *I* know'

Shobha, very polite, expressing the correct amount of restrained grief, asked, Did she suffer at the end?'

Radhica addressed instead the morose-looking man who had by now taken out a suitcase from the trunk and was holding it at his side, looking on absent-mindedly at his sisters. 'Vijay, you don't look too good. Be careful that you don't end up like Mammy, you know. She didn't suffer at all. She die so peacefully. Everything went so smooth,' she said ambiguously. 'If it wasn't for Ramlakhan and Oma and she husband, I don't know what would have happen.' Oma was her daughter, fat, and like the husband she had recently acquired, always grumpy and overdressed. 'They must be didn't sleep for these past few nights.'

'And what about you?' Vijay asked. 'You look very exhausted.'

She gave a tired little laugh, fanning her face with her handkerchief. 'That is my duty, boy Vijay. I can't complain. I only too glad that Mammy gone in a better world somewhere now.'

From a distance, Deo shouted, 'Radhica! That is Vijay and Shobha who come?'

'Look you all, go and talk to Daddy now. I still have a few things to arrange.'

'Okay. Don't overexert yourself,' Vijay told her. She sighed, the lines on the brow deepening.

They walked up the gently sloping hill where Deo and Uncle Seebaran were talking, Ramlakhan imprisoned between them.

Radhica called out wearily, 'Oma. All the pitch-pine split already? Make sure that it cut up in small pieces, okay, otherwise, it wouldn't burn.'

The tent had been constructed along the old estate house; the yard of the newer wooden structure was too muddy and uneven to accommodate the funeral. A few distant relatives, observing Deo, considered whether they should walk up the muddy path and offer their condolences. The pathway was daunting enough; they decided to leave Deo alone.

Radhica was supervising again, asking for more chairs, looking worried at the tarpaulin, testing the bamboo posts, watching the cotton cloth being cut into little square pieces and fitted into the split ends of two-foot long bamboo ends. She enquired about the amount of ghee, the colour of the flowers, the strength of the garlands. Not satisfied, she peered into the cardboard boxes, checking and rearranging.

Then someone shouted, 'She reach!'

A shrill echo emphasised the moment. 'She reach. Oh God, she really reach.'

Everyone got up, awaiting the arrival of the hearse. The lesser relatives removed themselves to the chairs at the back, the closer relatives: cousins, grandchildren, nieces and nephews, converged at the front.

The hearse stopped just at the entrance. Two very black middle-aged men took out the stretcher expertly, sliding it onto the prepared table.

'Careful it don't slide down,' Radhica said. 'The wheels might just take off.'

'No. No. It wouldn't do that,' one of the attendants said casually. 'The wheels come up and fold inside. Watch below and you will see.'

Oma was not convinced. 'Suppose it slip off. This table on a slope you know.'

The attendant tried to reassure her. He pushed the stretcher roughly. It did not move.

Her cheeks swelled. She looked angrily at the attendant.

Then someone at the back uttered a low, mournful cry, like a frightened horse whinnying. Everyone was shocked. The cry had come from a lesser relative. Those at the front looked back threateningly. But the crier was a very old woman, a regular figure at funerals. This gave her a special kind of right. The usurpation was forgiven. Then all at once, everyone began wailing. Oma, still riveted to the table, refusing to budge, began breathing heavily, her low-cut blouse emphasising each elaborate breath.

Radhica moaned, 'Calm down, Oma. I know you feeling it. You was always the favourite. But that gone now. Nobody could bring she back again.' The crowd reacted appropriately. There was a fresh wave of wailing. Then a hush descended slowly. A young woman with two chubby girls was walking up the hill. She was a niece, one of the closer relatives who had married someone of a different religion, had been divorced and was reputed to be living a wanton, reckless life. She came and seated herself at the front, near the entrance, arranging two chairs for the chubby girls.

Radhica said in a resigned tone, 'Oma, go and tell your grandfather to come and start the ceremony.'

Deo, barefooted, supported by his son and daughter, walked slowly to the tent.

He asked, 'Where Subhash and Devi?'

Shobha said, 'That is what I saying, Daddy. They couldn't get a flight in time. Me and Vijay were lucky.'

'Okay. Don't worry, *beti*. She dead now. It wouldn't make any difference.'

At the entrance he stopped. Shobha nudged him gently. Inside, Radhica, fanning herself, said, 'Come and sit down on this chair over here. The pundit waiting on you.'

'You all go and see your mother for the last time,' he said to Shobha and Vijay. 'I will stay here for the time.' Both seemed reluctant to leave him, to look at the coffin, to look at the face they had not seen for more than ten years. Shobha looked at the ground, avoiding the face. When she was alongside she looked up and, for a moment, she seemed more confused than sad. Then she ran her fingers over her mother's hair, her forehead, her nose, lingering over the flowers that had been placed over the chest and neck. Vijay stood at the other end, massaging the toes and ankles. Staring straight ahead, he looked as impassive as ever, but teardrops were running down his cheeks and falling on his frail hands. Radhica came and placed her hands around his shoulder, understanding his sorrow, as she had understood him years ago when they were children. The lesser relatives at the back peered through the crowd, pressing and squeezing. The closer relatives knew that close as they were, this was something denied everyone else but the husband and the children. And they knew that this was no show. Now there were no dramatic mournful cries, just the silent grief of three children. And coming through this grief, a bond that never existed before and which, in a short while, would exist no more. They looked towards their father, wanting him to come, insisting that he participate in this closeness. Perhaps he understood this, but the same stubborn pride that had provoked so many of the calamities that had beset him in the past, now insisted that he remain apart, a spectator rather than a participant. Some of the lesser relatives, remembering his decision to take his wife away from the comfortable estate house, felt that he was responsible for her death, that she had begun to die since that time, that his distance was dictated by guilt rather than by pride.

The pundit cleared his throat, signalling that he was ready to begin. Oma seized the opportunity, telling the pundit in a simpering, grieving voice, 'Before you begin, I would like to read a few lines from the Gita. Is the only thing that keep me from breaking down these last few days.'

'No!' Deo shouted from outside the tent. 'No! What stupidness is this!' Oma shrank back, her fat cheeks jiggling, trembling with consternation and anger.

Radhica said, 'Don't mind him, Oma, is the grief speaking, not you granddaddy. You know you was always his favourite.'

He interrupted. 'We have procedures to follow and this is not one of them. If everybody went and read this and that, when we will leave here? Tomorrow? Next week? Let the pundit begin with his discourse. He is the one trained to do that, no one else.'

The pundit, young, and now very nervous, began in a high-pitched voice, but realised that this voice was permissible in a funeral because it could be put down to choked grief rather than to nervousness. He droned on and on about her virtuous qualities, emphasising her ability to bear sacrifices and still retain her cheerful nature. He spoke of her early life, growing up with her step-father, married when she was yet a child, working in the cocoa estate in Flanagan Town, then the sugar cane estate in Buen Intento, living briefly in Chaguanas when the business became prosperous, then leaving Chaguanas as the problems set in, still smiling as before. 'She was a faithful companion over all these years, never making any complain at all.'

'She had nothing to complain about. As long as she was by my side she had every reason to be happy.'

Shobha said, in a soothing voice, 'Okay Daddy, he didn't mean that. Let the discourse continue.' She looked at her wristwatch.

In a less calm manner, Radhica said, 'Leave him alone, Shobha. Let the grief come out. This is his way.' Shobha's son gazed disinterestedly at the coffin, rubbing his eyes.

'She was good to me. Nobody could question that. And in my own way, I was equally good to her. Nobody should question that either.'

'We all know that, Daddy, but let the pundit continue or we will all be late for the cremation.'

'Oh God.' Radhica began to fan herself angrily. 'What going on. What really going on. Don't mind that, Oma. This was bound to happen.' Oma, unexpectedly thrust into the limelight, puffed out her cheeks, irritation plastered all over her face.

'It serve them right,' Oma said spitefully, directing her malice at no one in particular. In the meantime, Deo was being led by Uncle Seebaran back to the wooden house, up the muddy track..

He was saying, 'If she was here today, she would understand what I was saying. She alone could understand me. But let the pundit continue. That is his job. He doing a good job. Let him continue.' And in a fatherly tone he shouted, 'Don't worry,

THE FUNERAL

Shobha. We will reach at the cremation site in time. We wouldn't keep your mother waiting on this last journey.'

Then it was time to replace the coffin on the hearse.

'Vijay, you and Ramlakhan help over there. Hold that end,' Radhica instructed.

The pundit interrupted. 'Let Ramlakhan stay here. The son-in-law is not suppose to handle the coffin.'

'Don't worry, Pa. I will hold the coffin for you. I will take your place.' The cheeks seemed ready to burst.

In the car following the hearse, Radhica sat with her head bowed, humming a mournful tune. Ramlakhan tried to drive as carefully as was possible, steering away from all the pot-holes. Someone in the back honked a horn.

'Drive, Ramlack. You just be careful,' Radhica told him. Oma rolled up the glass window.

In another vehicle, Shobha was telling Vijay how much things had changed; every now and again she would stop to point out something to her son. 'That across there is the chimney,' she said. And that is the factory where cane is ground and the juice convened into sugar.'

'Can I get some?' he asked.

You remember the molasses?' she said, speaking now to Vijay. 'How Mummy had always given it to us. I really hated the taste but she knew how good it was for us to take it.

He shook his head sadly.

'Is that Grandpa in that car over there?' Shobha's son asked.

'Yes. Wave to him. Oh, it's all right, he's not looking back. He and Uncle Seebaran were always very close,' she said, speaking once more to Vijay.

Deo was talking to Uncle Seebaran, who was driving. 'I will open a girls' boarding school in her memory. She always wanted me to do that.'

Uncle Seebaran, understanding him as no one else did, said,

'You start building all these castles again? As far as I recall, she never mention anything about any girls school.'

'Only at the end she start speaking about this. It will be a big school, painted in blue and white and the dormitory will be just at the back, right next to the playground. In the middle of this I will build a shrine with her statue and every morning, just before classes start, all the girls will line up there for their morning prayers. Later on I might build a complete temple.'

'Where you going to build this school?'

'Next to my small house, where I could keep an eye on everything and everybody.'

'And what the girls will eat? You building any restaurant or parlour. Maybe every morning and evening you will let them out and allow them to graze. Clean up the cane field in no time.'

'I have to accomplish that before I pass on. The trouble with you, Seebaran, is that you always thinking too small. You always content to be a hardware owner. That is your whole life. When last you pray to God?'

Uncle Seebaran, understanding this mood, changed the subject. 'Now is a good time to consider dividing up the land, otherwise everything will just go to the Government.'

'The minute I start dividing, they will be at each other's throats. Let the Government take it.'

'You should discuss this with Shobha and Vijay.'

'You want me to discuss this with them? They just born yesterday and now I have to ask them for advice?'

'Is your own children.'

'I know is my own children. You know what Shobha brought for me? You was hearing? Bottles and bottles of tablets and vitamins.' He laughed. 'I know she really care, but tell me, you expect me to take all those things? Look. Feel here.' He flexed his biceps. 'Tablet and vitamins didn't build this you know. Is hard work and a good mind. The absence of any kind of vice whatsoever.'

At the cremation site Deo walked towards the rail at the edge of the asphalt ground, where the sea hung below a sheer drop of about fifty feet, the waves curling around the broken-off pieces of shale and unburned pitch-pine. He remained there while the mixture of rice, ghee, and sugar was placed on the coffin, while the pundit performed his rites, while the pieces of bamboo were placed around the pyre, while the fires were lit.

Then, feeling the heat and seeing the smoke coiling towards the sea and then blown back inland, he turned around and walked slowly towards a group of old men who were silently contemplating the scene. For the first time he looked exhausted, devoid of all vitality.

Vijay was rubbing his eyes. After a while he moved away from the smoke. Shobha was pointing to the fire and explaining something to her son, the other hand on his shoulder.

Radhica stood close to the fire, her hands clasped behind her back, her eyes fixed on the flame. Ramlakhan touched her arm, asking her to step away. She seemed not to hear him. He left and joined Oma and her husband who were in a car parked on the grassy lawn, just at the entrance to the cremation site.

Another funeral arrived, the loud speaker blaring its mournful bhajan. A few of the lesser relatives looked anxiously at Deo, afraid that he might make some complaint and disrupt the soothing solemnity of the occasion. But Deo was occupied, busily explaining something to a very old, stooped man with a long, flowing beard.

And then it was over, everyone leaving; their grief washed away.

Shobha told her son, 'So you see how your grandparents and their friends were smart? When you burn someone, you can't see anything again and all the grieving is displaced immediately. Now if your grandma was buried, wouldn't you be thinking tomorrow about the state of her body and the day after, about whether the worms were already coming?'

He asked her, 'Mummy, can we stop somewhere and get an iced drink?'

She told him, 'Shh. I want you to remember everything so when Daddy asks you to write a report you would be able to record everything that you saw.'

The next day there was a memorial service. All the close relatives were present. The service, held in the older estate house, started late. Everyone had some special memory to recall, something to prove how close they had been, how much she had held a special place for each of them. When he arrived, indifferently dressed, they were still misty-eyed with nostalgia.

He spoke of his early life — hardly mentioning her — and of the strict discipline that had shaped his career and his moral beliefs. He quoted from religious texts, related several anecdotes and then began to moralise about the decaying standard of decency that he saw around him. He became philosophical, obscure, and angry.

One or two of the relatives left, making some excuse. He seemed not to notice. When he mentioned his plans to build the girls' boarding school, a couple more left.

'In the cane field right in the back is where I going to construct the school. Bit by bit I will construct this school and if nobody want to help, then I will do it alone. I accustomed to hard work. That is no stranger to me. And you all probably notice how many important people were at the funeral yesterday. Well all these people will contribute something to the building of this school even though, looking at your faces now, I know that you feel that it is impossible. And that is the trouble with you all. You have no vision. That is why none of you will succeed in anything. When last anybody here read from the religious texts?'

'Not everybody have the time to do this, Daddy. You have to understand that everybody working. I try to put in a few hours every night but you know how tiring it is. I wouldn't like to ask anybody else to have to go through that.' Radhica gave her tired, little laugh.

'Is not something to put up with. The minute you start thinking it is a burden, then you shouldn't do it all. I can't pass a day without it. Nobody force me. I read the books because of the lessons I learn. Whenever anybody disagree with something that I do, it is very easy for me to refer them to some chapter or the other. That is how I always live my life and how I will continue to live it.' He spoke slower now, emphasising each word. 'And all my readings show me that there is nothing wrong with getting a woman who is past the childbearing age and without any children to become a companion.'

'You should not be saying these things, Daddy.'

'I am very serious. Try to understand my point of view.' And looking at him, Shobha realised that he was serious.

A few more of the relatives, feeling either embarrassed or angry, decided to leave.

'Mammy only cremate yesterday and you talking like this now?'

Ramlakhan tried unsuccessfully to match her injured look.

'At your age?' Vijay asked.

'Don't worry about age. I didn't say that I would remarry. The word I use is companion. Somebody to cook and wash and do simple duties.'

'We could arrange for a maid,' Shobha told him.

'No maid. This companion must be a person who I could talk with and discuss things.'

'Is really an audience you want, then,' Uncle Seebaran said, attempting to sound casual, but with a sharp edge of irritation in his voice.

'You should not try to replace Mummy in this fashion, and not so soon,' Shobha said.

'Look I going now. Mummy and Daddy, you will meet me in the car.' Oma stood up roughly, the chair clattering against the concrete.

'What will people say?' Uncle Seebaran asked him, angrily now.

'What people say is irrelevant. How I feel is more important.'

'But to be thinking like this so soon after, Daddy?'

'Mummy! You coming or not? I not going to stay here and listen to this.'

'Wait, Oma. We coming now.'

'Go! Go everybody.' Go and don't come back in this place again. Everybody leave me here.' For a moment it seemed as though his voice would crack but then he composed himself. 'My thoughts are always pure. It is the dirtiness in your own minds that creating this lack of understanding. Go back to your happy, healthy life and leave me here alone.' He got up, holding the edge of the table for support. 'Leave me alone and let me go to that old broken down house. I will sleep there alone tonight with nobody to disturb me.' He walked slowly up the hill, up the muddy pathway. 'Go back to your nice family and leave the old man alone.'

After almost everyone else had left, Shobha asked Uncle Seebaran, 'Do you think that someone should go and perhaps speak with him?'

'Suppose he do something stupid. Remember, he alone up there in that house,' Radhica said.

'Don't be stupid,' Uncle Seebaran told her. 'He is the last person to do anything stupid like what you thinking.'

'And what about that stupid thing he just talk about,' she insisted.

'I think he's making a jackass of himself,' Vijay said suddenly. They looked at him with surprise. Then slowly some of his indignation seeped into each of them.

'How could Daddy even think of such a thing?'

'Another woman sleeping where my own grandma use to sleep.'

'I know how you feel, Oma, but he will only do that over my dead body.'

'You think he will listen to you?' Uncle Seebaran asked with a sudden interest.

Radhica, making the statement more as a demonstration of her anger than as an indication of her power, said uncertainly, 'And even if he do it, I don't think I will ever talk to him again or cross that gap again.'

'When I leave Trinidad this time, I am doubtful that I would return again.'

'There is really nothing to return for. Everything is gone now,' Vijay said.

For the three days before they returned home, Vijay and Shobha stayed at a cousin's house. They avoided speaking of their father. Most of the time, Vijay sat in a bentwood rocking chair, blowing into his handkerchief and rocking slowly. Shobha visited the Zoo, the Botanic Gardens and the Pitch Lake. After each visit she reminded her son that he would have to write a report for his daddy when he returned home.

And Deo did indeed acquire a companion, a cross, haggard-looking old woman. She stayed with him for exactly five days, then left cursing and quarrelling.

Months passed. He aged rapidly. The face, often unshaven for weeks, became slacker, the jaw looser. His once strong hands became loose and wrinkled. As his debts grew, the workmen left one by one. And then he was alone, walking barefooted through the mud; stooped now, with a hoe or cutlass in his hand, going to the fields in the early morning and returning late in the evening. He had always told his children that it was his wish that he should die in the fields, alone and peacefully. Then, the idea was drawn out of romance, now it looked as though his wish would be granted. Dying in the field, not peacefully, but alone and forlorn.

At Christmas, Radhica, forgetting her earlier promise, visited him. She brought an aluminium container filled with food and some small plastic containers with sweets. He was in the field and she awaited his return; Ramlakhan, in the car, was waiting impatiently. When she saw her father limping, his body bent, she was horrified. He opened the latch and she followed him in, placing the containers on a table. She surveyed the dilapidated house with the same feeling of horror, observing the empty table, the one broken chair, the bare mattress on the bed, the unswept floor.

'Where the stove and all the furniture, Daddy?'

Not answering her, he hobbled to the bed, lying and staring at the rough, criss-crossed rafters and at the spaces between the aluminium sheets.

'Who cooking for you? What you eating?' Outside, in the car, Ramlakhan honked the car horn. 'Maybe I should leave the old stove, that nobody using at home, over here. I can't understand what you does be eating all the time.' She saw the sooty-looking bananas and the orange peels on a shelf. She felt a sadness drawn partly from guilt, but also from the fact that the effects of all her previous kindness and care had fallen into decay.

He spoke in a slow, steady voice. 'Long time ago, there use to be children playing all around here. Jumping on the truck tray

THE FUNERAL

and pretending to drive the tractor and running through the field. Nobody playing here again.'

When the breeze blew through the holes on the wall where the window had once been, she smelt the unwashed clothes, piled at the side of the bed and the dust rising from the floor. She felt that she was smelling a place where no one lived anymore, smelling just emptiness and death.

'Let me dust out the bed for you. Just get up for a minute.'

Waiting for an answer, she observed his irregular, choked breathing and realised that he was asleep. The breeze blew through the house. She hurried away.

In the car, on their way back, Ramlakhan said, 'So how the old hermit going? He plant any banyan tree to meditate under or tame any wild animals yet?' Seeing her concern, he added, 'Well, he must be finally happy now because this is just the kind of life he always wanted to live. He alone, living in peace.'

She nodded her head slowly.

On the bare mattress, the old man Deo, dreamt of little children sliding down the trucks, running about in the fields, and he with the smallest one straddled on his back, running after them, shouting with mock anger. In a clearing in the canefield, piles of bricks, lumber and steel lay around the statue of a woman with a smiling face.

JOHN FITZGERALD TENNYSON

He hated beggars, the way they would select him in a crowd, boldly walking up, demanding money. Spotting him from a distance, they would bypass everyone else and come to him. Who the hell I is, he thought bitterly: the King of England? In less angry moments he felt he knew why he was always the brunt of all the assaults. He was sure it was his small, dark body, the exceedingly plain features, the walk that suggested weakness and vulnerability — the hands stiff, never moving when he walked.

After a while he resisted.

'Mister, gimme a dollar to buy something to eat please. I didn't eat nothing for the whole day.'

'In some countries, people does fast for weeks. Remain hungry. Is good for you.'

Sometimes they would run up to him, proffering a paper signed by a doctor, detailing some serious ailment — invariably heart problems — and the expenditure that would be needed for the treatment or for an overseas operation. He would stare at the paper, creased so often that it was soft and fragile, and at the doctor's hasty scrawl and understand the scam. Then he would look at the child's face: the dirt, the injured, demanding look, the carefully prepared grief and feel a rage boiling within him. He would not merely refuse or shout out his anger, but would pretend interest, uncovering the layers of deceit, one by one. 'And what is the name of the doctor?'

'I can't read,' the thin, reedy voice would say.

'Where your mother living right now?'

'On the pavements, sometimes under the stores,' the voice would whisper correctly.

'How much this operation costing?'

Dirty fingers would point somewhere in the paper. 'It mark down right here.'

'Is a expensive operation. Like she very sick?'

Eyes would look to the ground, fingers tugging at the ends of frayed trousers.

'Okay, I will tell you what. I have a friend who is a doctor in the hospital. Let we go and talk to him now.'

The fingers would snatch the paper; the injured grief replaced by a sniping hate.

And he would smile in triumph.

At other times, realising that he had made a misjudgement, he would quietly give a shilling or two. But this was rare. There was nothing miserly or cold about him; what really rankled was the feeling that he presented such a tempting appearance, that he was forever cast in the role of someone to be nibbled at.

It was this same feeling that made him such a bad driver on the roads. And he, regarding the resulting curses as another sign of his insignificance, would drive even more recklessly, eliciting even more curses. He would always accelerate whenever someone tried to overtake. If a car he was following stopped too often, he would pass the car and then drive very slowly, increasing the speed of his vehicle only when he suspected that the driver behind was shifting into a high gear. The worst offenders, though, the ones he could bear the least, were those who stopped without flicking on the indicator lights on their vehicle. This was especially so of taxi-drivers, and he began to wonder whether they were a species apart; a group which had not evolved sufficiently to enable them to handle mechanical tasks. He would apply the brake suddenly and come to a screeching stop just a few inches behind the offending car, causing the taxi-driver to look back in concern and curse.

Once he had gone to the Licensing Office to state his complaints. The male clerk, frustrated at the indifference of a newly appointed female clerk, winked at her, offering this unexpected intrusion as his special gift. She, directed thus, noticed the worried face, the stiff hands, the incongruous blend of colour in the clothing, and then the face again, at the upper lip trembling nervously. She smiled shyly. The male clerk moved his chair closer to hers.

The Licensing Office suddenly felt small, hot and suffocating. He stormed out, stumbling on the steps.

He lived with his mother in an unpainted, wooden house that sloped down on the left corners, where a step built with boards of uneven strength and hardness tilted erratically towards the rotten, wooden railings. The yard was always dirty and weeds grew among the water barrels and the zinnia and marigold flowers that sprung in small hesitant patches. Beneath the house, which was supported by six concrete posts, a clothes line made of old electrical wire was always laden with clothes and sheets billowing like wind-laden sails. Within all of the clothes would be his mother swinging slowly in a hammock, her eyes closed but hearing everything around her: the neighbours quarrelling, the dogs barking, and a young girl singing in a house across the road. He hated having to return to the house and he would hurry from the car, walking with care up the steps, into the kitchen, hearing the loosened boards creaking as he stepped gingerly on them.

Then he would lock himself securely in his room. He always felt surprised when he entered his room, mentally remarking how different it looked from the rest of the house. The walls were painted in aquamarine which, he had read in a magazine, could induce a feeling of tranquillity. He had, however, made a concession and painted the area where the window had previously been, in red, learning also from the magazine that red was the colour of aggression and could heighten a person's physical energy. Too much tranquillity could be a damn dangerous thing, he thought.

Everything was neat: the framed pictures of himself as a baby and as a young man, the plastic pipe resting on two nails over which he had draped his clothing, the old, sturdy electric fan on the dressing table next to the hair brushes, combs and an assortment of deodorants: everything was in its proper place; everything was orderly.

He never allowed his mother to clean his room, afraid that she might stumble across some confession he had written in his diary or learn some secret, painful thing about him. He never really spoke with her, not because of any quarrel or ill feeling, but because their conversations always tired him. There were times though, when he would return from some newly acquired work, or when he had just been dismissed and wanted sympathy, and then he would be rebuffed by her own long tirades: her rheumatism, her failing eyesight and then to less personal woes such as the house's shifting foundations and problems over money. Seeing her swinging slowly in the hammock, the heels out of the slippers from digging into the concrete, he knew that the afflictions she complained of were real. But they exhausted him, and he was never able to respond in an encouraging manner.

After a while he stopped expecting any sympathy and she continued with her rocking.

Before he found steady employment with the bank, he had tried many other kinds of work. He had worked for two months in a Chinese restaurant, owned not by a Chinese, but by a large, red, fierce-looking, curly-haired man called Hamel. His job was to chop up the vegetables and throw them into the huge cauldron. He liked to hear the hissing sound and would step away quickly to avoid the small specks of oil ricocheting off the pot; smiling at the cook, who was Chinese and who dealt with the meats. The cook would look harassed and unfriendly, not encouraging any conversation.

But after a while the routine became boring. One day he saw a special recipe section in a magazine he had bought. Flicking through the pages he decided that his luck was in. He remembered reading about a woman from America who had, just before her return flight, purchased a magazine at the airport and, weeks later, realised that the stub on the inside cover had enabled her to win an Oldsmobile, a computer and a variety of other American goodies. Reading the recipes, he was convinced of his own good luck. A bouquet garni —how exotic the words sounded! Sprigs of parsley and a spray of thyme. The words sprang out, delicious already. Casserole! Sauté! Puree! His mind was set. He would show the old Chinese cook. Goodies of all different flavours and aromas filtered through his mind.

He was fired the next day. Mr. Hamel said, 'You want the business to go bust?' He pointed to the sign just above the doorway. 'What that sign say, not Chinese restaurant? Tell me if this looking like anything that any self-respecting Chinese will eat.' He motioned to the limp, lifeless hash of vegetables and noodles that clung desperately to each other in the pot. The recipe, so exciting in the magazine, had not been a success.

'At least I don't taste the food all the time while it still cooking and be dribbling all over the pot,' he said spitefully. The cook busied himself with his stirring, throwing in a fresh set of vegetables, the noise exploding in the kitchen.

Other jobs ended up in a somewhat similar fashion, but the one that brought the biggest feeling of disgust was the time spent at the Caura Hospital, a convalescent home for asthmatic patients and those suffering from diseases of the lung. At first the work promised much. On his way to the wards, carrying the bundles of folded linen smelling of camphor, he would sing to the tune of a popular calypso, a song he had composed:

'Asthmatic, bronchitic, pneumatic
I just love to treat the sick
I shoulda be a doctor instead
But excuse me while I clean up the bed.'

And then he was transferred to another department.

Instead of replacing the dirty pillow cases and sheets with fresh, clean-smelling ones and chatting cheerfully with the patients, he had to clean the floor and the face basins. The floors were not really bad but the basins terrified him, leaving his stomach churning and protesting. Encountering greenish-yellowish sputum quivering like an alien in a science fiction movie, or realising that he had misjudged his swipe with the foamy cleaning sponge and that some of the red-tinged phlegm had latched onto his fingers, he would shrivel up in disgust, holding his hand away, thinking of disease and amputation. Whenever that happened he would have to wash his own vomit from the basin.

And the patients, once so much his friends, now seemed like impostors, cajoling him with their infirmities and then springing all this nastiness upon him. He had always listened attentively while the doctors were explaining, 'What you have is crepitations rather than wheezing. Listen carefully. Breathe in now. You see? Your sounds are finer. Not coarse at all. The rhomchi sound.'

He started treating the patients roughly. 'What happen, you can't get up from the bed any faster? Eh? They stick you down last night?' He would look closely at the sheet. 'No. No glue here. Then it must be the rhomchi.' The word infuriated him. 'Not rhomchi, romki. You know why?' he pressed his face closer to the startled patient. 'Is because only donkey does get romki. That is why.' The patient's look of helplessness would bring a short, dry laugh, but remembering the disgusting things associated with this helplessness he would become angry once more. 'Is you who does be nastying up the sink all the time? Is you! Don't feel that I don't know.' Then the anger would shift into a sort of incredulous disgust. He would stare at the small, wizened body. 'What I can't understand is how a small person like you does bring up all them nasty things. Where it does fit? Where?'

Reported to the hospital officials by the patients, he was summoned to the head office. Listening to the accusations, he gazed around, believing for a moment that the doctor was referring to someone else. He heard him speaking of a person who was inconsiderate, useless, maladjusted and malicious; he concentrated on the humming air-conditioner. He looked at the machine, observing the knobs, the brand name written in fancy letters, and the broken concrete around the edges. He followed the copper tubing to a small hole at the other end of the room. He barely heard the doctor saying, 'The most no-good employee that ever work in this hospital. Abusing sick people in this manner!'

Outside, on the busy street, while surveying the pedestrians walking languidly, a doubles vendor expertly wrapping the doubles in brown paper with a flick of the wrist; seeing the hungry faces, throats swallowing expectantly, the rage came, suffusing him with its energy and then with its uselessness. He walked across the street, his arms stiffer than ever. A driver honked his horn. He walked slower, contemplating the curses. Why he didn't bounce me down? Nobody would care. In the morning the rubbish truck will just collect me together with all the other rubbish and the dead dogs and carry me to the La Basse.

He walked into an old, crowded rumshop and ordered a beer. The liquid, golden and appealing in the bottle, tasted stale in his mouth. He drank it swiftly slowing his breath, trying to stifle the taste. He bought another and sipped slowly now, the taste becoming more remote. The bartender came to him, removed the empty bottle, wiped the table with a damp rag and went back to the counter.

He looked at the bartender more carefully: the pudgy features, the drooping arms, and tried to decipher some frustration, some disillusionment he might have felt with this line of work. But the dull, unintelligent face intruded, destroying the picture. And then, suddenly, he felt out of place. Like a stranger. A middle-aged man came and sat by his table, staring at him every now and again, shaking his glass, allowing the ice to cool the rum. The man's presence made him feel uncomfortable, then irritated.

The man said in a drunken slur, 'When I go home tonight, wifey will give me plenty horrors.'

He said nothing.

'Horrors day and night.' The drunk drew closer, leaning over the table. 'One day I will show she who is the boss. And then she will either have to shape up or move out. Lock, stock and barrel.'

He drank the beer quickly forcing the liquid down his throat.

'You married too, boss?'

He shook his head, feeling the hastily drunk beer burning his stomach.

'Well, let me tell you something. Don't get involved in that. Don't ever get involved in that business. Wifey and them just design to make trouble.' The drunk shook his glass slowly, watching the ice swirl around the rum. 'Is only problems, left, right and centre. Who will believe that I use to be the happiest man before?'

From behind the counter the bartender shouted, 'Asevero! I tired tell you to stop disturbing the blasted customers.'

The glass slammed the table. 'You see how he does talk to me? You see the respect he have for me? But let him continue. He will regret all that. I stop arguing now. I just peaceful and quiet, but one day when I sitting down here quiet and anybody interfere with me, I go just spring up and start ramajaying. Tear up everybody left, right and centre.' Sensing the absurdity of this fantasy he relapsed once more. 'One day he will find out.' The eyelids blinked slowly like a frog's. 'One day,' he repeated, 'one day I will show him. I will show everybody.'

He smelt the rum mingled with urine from the opened door at the side of the bar, saw the drooping eyes on the drunk's face, the down-turned mouth that would never hold any threat, the palms convulsively tapping the table like a dying man's final movements, and left hurriedly.

Driving back home, he shut one eye to stave off the drunken double vision. Later he cursed the tilting step and the creaking boards.

Then he got the work in the bank. The application had been written with exaggerated care, detailing his addiction to the world of high finance and his burning desire to work in the investment-oriented sector — phrases gleaned from magazines. The advertisement in the newspaper had stated that the applicant should possess a car. He thought of his old, yellow, Datsun 1600 and decided to spruce up the vehicle, mentioning not the paste-ridden body or the faulty alternator and the worn down shocks but, rather untruthfully, the equaliser, the sunroof, the sheepskin seat covers and the air-conditioning system.

After a very brief interview, he was given the job. The Monday morning that he started working, clad in his green bell-bottomed trousers, his pink shirt and yellow tie, he told his mother, 'I have to hurry this morning. I get this big work in the bank.' She rocked slowly, saying nothing.

His job was a combination of caddie-boy, chauffeur, messenger and door-opener. He shuttled between various departments, delivering messages, making sure that the catering service had the drinks prepared for the tea break and the food for the midday meal.

Initially, he was never confronted by the subservience of the work; beneath him there was a whole plethora of lesser workers he could order about. 'What? The tea not ready yet. When I should pass back for it? Tomorrow? Next week? Just remember that it have other caterers in the place, you know.' Or, 'Mr. Chee-Mook say that he want this faxed right now. What you mean you busy?' He would use words like that: faxed, Xeroxed, data and modules. Passing the cashiers and the loans officers he would gaze longingly at the computers and at the green letters and figures appearing so quickly and efficiently on the monitors.

He purchased computer magazines and, very casually, he would mention something about bytes and software or about his disc drive at home, or about the new printer he had acquired. The cashiers receiving the Xeroxed papers would gaze at him in astonishment.

For a while, he was happy enjoying the quiet nods of approval he got when he had brought in a file for the accountant, and the moments when he would berate the caterers for their indifference. But most of all, he enjoyed the reserved area in the bank's car park, meant for him and no one else. He would look at the area shaped like a parallelogram and at the white lines separating his reserved area from the manager's. Once or twice, he felt like writing his name on the spot. Eventually he wrote, in small, white letters, the number of his car: PR 9967.

He became friendly with the bank's security guard, Stewart, who treated him with courtesy and respect. He felt that he saw in Stewart the ambitions that had, at one time, characterised his own life. Sometimes, after work, he would give Stewart a lift to his home and he was always impressed when he saw the modest but well-kept place: the lawn clipped neatly, the small fence of kora shrubs, and the pruned Julie mango tree shading the small, painted, concrete flat. Sometimes Stewart would invite him in but he would remain on the verandah, drinking fruit juice and commenting on the appearance of the shrubbery and flowers. Stewart was always pleased by that and he would talk with great expertise of the grafted fruit trees and the different soil types and pH balance that suited the varieties of flowers he had planted.

Looking through the curtains, he would observe the children, well-mannered and formal, sitting erect on the long couch, nibbling away at cakes, or fruits collected from the backyard, while looking at television.

Then he would hear their mother saying, 'Okay, Jonathan and Joshua and Mary, is time to start your home lesson now. Turn off the TV.' And they would place the cake or fruit on the little china plates and troop off to the table.

Stewart would look contented. He would say, 'We have to make the best of what we have. I try to bring out some discipline in them.'

'They looking like little bank manager and accountant already.'

They would both laugh and talk about the wantonness of the children nowadays. Stewart would shake his head. 'It have no ambition again. Ambition like it leave this country and gone to live somewhere else.' Stewart would smile, then becoming more serious would say, 'You know how much people does envy me. They does say that I too serious and that I should loosen up a bit.' He looked at Stewart: black and stocky, hair neatly clipped, a solemn expression almost always on his face and found it difficult to imagine him loosening up. 'No time for that. I living now for the children.'

Stewart, in his forties, just five years or so older than him and speaking with such seriousness and with all these plans for his children. Sometimes being with Stewart depressed him.

'I thinking about getting married too, but I trying to stock up the little egg nest first. Have to build up first.'

Stewart would nod solemnly, missing the desperate apology.

When he saw his mother rocking in the hammock, her eyes closed, he told her, 'I thinking about renovating this place. Fix them creaking boards and the steps too.' The rocking continued.

She was mildly surprised when, one week later, a Leyland diesel truck deposited a load of specially treated imported pine and five thick mahogany planks on a clump of etiolated zinnias.

She was less surprised when the weeds slowly overran the pile of pine and mahogany and occasionally she would sit up from the hammock to shout at the neighbour's mongrel that had staked its claim to the area, stretched on the top of the pile of treated lumber, sunning itself. Returning to the hammock she would mutter, 'Trouble and more trouble.'

About a month after, this aspect of her trouble was removed.

One night the treated lumber was stolen.

One day, on the verandah with Stewart, listening to him speak about some mosaic virus that was affecting several kinds of fruit trees on the island, he said suddenly, 'I taking this computer course. Correspondence. Real expensive, but it worth it.'

Stewart mentioned that computer programming was an important field and that he had high hopes for his children in that direction.

'I might have to leave the bank.'

Stewart looked grave. 'That is the way of the world. You have to climb up the ladder. You can't stick up on one rung.'

'It real tough, but I feel that I have the talent for it.'

'Maybe you could give Jonathan some lessons. I feel that he have the talent for it too.'

He changed the topic.

One of the cashiers at the bank was a pink, rosy-faced girl whose name he did not know. He would see her counting the money, a serious, deliberate look on her face and feel a tenderness towards her. Sometimes when a shop-keeper or grocer had deposited a cellophane bags filled with copper and silver coins, he would observe her exhaustion and feel sympathy when she blew on her palms, rubbing the fingers against each other. Once, when he was delivering a sheaf of type-written papers to the accountant, he saw her conferring with the loans officer, sitting in the little cubicle next to him. He saw the monitor on her desk displaying the green figures. The bank was busy that day and no one took notice of him when he stood before her monitor; staring at the display on the screen. He remembered an article in the computer magazine saying that a computer was, in many ways, like your personal slave. Give it the right commands and it obeyed instantly. He tried to recall some of the commands. He typed, load, goto and other things he remembered. Then he typed his name: John Fitzgerald Tennyson. The letters on the keyboard felt soft and cushiony, springing back into place after being depressed. The computer responded. The display faded from the screen. Feeling uneasy now he pressed various symbols and combinations, waiting for the display to reappear. He became aware of another cashier, a tall, Amazon-like woman named Mrs. Alphonso, staring at him.

When he was summoned to the office of the assistant-manager, Mr. Lezama, all the excuses that he had earlier concocted evaporated: re-adjusting the key-board, mechanical failure, electrical failure, Alphonso really responsible. In his mind he saw the excuses streaming away, each one printed on a banner tugged by an aeroplane and its spiteful pilot.

Mr. Lezama was livid. 'Who the hell tell you to interfere with the apparatus?'

He hung his head.

'You know anything about an apparatus like that? You know how much that apparatus cost?'

He was reminded of the scene in the doctor's office at the Caura Hospital. He looked around the office, searching for diversions. But the office was too scant, devoid of air-conditioning units, devoid of anything that could hold his interest. The bland, maroon, felt-covered walls were too bare and unfamiliar. In any case, Mr. Lezama, unlike the doctor, was shouting — his voice probably reaching everybody in the bank. A brief spurt of anger came and then faded. He was afraid to look at Mr. Lezama.

'Is only because we have no prior complaints that we not releasing you this time.'

Releasing me? For a moment he thought of fowls being released from their coops and fluttering all over the bank. *I look like a fowl to him?*

'Now go back and don't let me hear any nonsense about you

again. Otherwise.'

Otherwise he will release me like a fowl, he thought bitterly. Like a layer that stop laying.

After work, walking out of the bank, he was accosted by a beggar, old but still sturdy-looking. 'Look. Haul you mangy old ass away from me, you hear. You think I is a assistant manager or something? You think that all I does do is play with apparatus whole day?'

Later in the car, driving home with Stewart, the rage remained with him. Stewart had said, in his soothing voice, 'That is the way, boy. You have to understand these off-white people.'

The car lurched to the left. 'Off-white? Off-white! You think is a paint? Off-white, cherry-white, apple-white? They playing off-white over here but let them go to America or England and see if they don't have to bunch up with black-skin people like me and you. Let them go to South Africa and play off-white and see if they don't line them up in a damn paint shop.'

'Is true,' Stewart said. 'But over here is over here. Who give you the work in the bank?' The rage fell away. He knew that Stewart was right. People in that position always take advantage, he thought, no matter what their colour is.

'Talking like I don't have me own apparatus at home,' he said, calmly now.

Locked securely in his room, he looked at his thin, dark, hairless hands. Maybe if I was fatter and whiter, nobody would dare speak to me like that. Or hairier. He passed the other hand on his arm, rubbing it softly. That night he dreamt of an encounter with Mr. Lezama and the rosy-cheeked girl. In the dream, while they were replacing their clothes, they saw him and laughed heartily, Mr. Lezama pulling the supple-looking girl closer to him, pointing and snickering. He felt revolted by the dream.

That same week he enrolled in an evening class as a computer programming student. When he went to register on the third floor of a building that was secreted between a Catholic Church and a police station, he almost changed his mind. The secretary, plump and alert, barely noticed him. She pushed some registration forms towards him, not looking up from the other forms she was re-checking.

'How much the class will cost?' he asked uncertainly.

'Four hundred dollars.'

'What about if I stay only for one term. I already have a little experience.'

'Where do you work?'

'In a bank. I does handle the apparatus all the time.'

'Anyways, you can't sign up for just one term. You have to take the entire year;' she said in a serious voice.

She got up and removed some square brown cards from a filing cabinet. She was fatter than he had originally assessed.

'If you think its too expensive...'

'Expensive? Not at all.' He had the money in his hands. It was too late.

In the first class he realised that he had made a mistake. There were twelve students in the class and he was relieved to note that at least two of them were older than him. But the magazines had given him the wrong picture. The computer resolutely refused to become an obedient, life-like servant, responding to his slightest touch or his friendly companion for various amusing games.

There was nothing amusing about the classes and his mind would reel with obscure, esoteric terms that seemed far less daunting in the magazines where he could proceed at his own pace, relaxed and unhurried by the serious, cynical teacher. He had always hated mathematics and now he realised, to his dismay, that this was an integral aspect of the course. He began to feel exhausted in the classes, at times on the verge of falling asleep. The teacher duly noted this. He was asked all kinds of nebulous questions. He dodged, parried and spluttered. The rest of the class grew impatient.

The building also housed an aerobics gymnasium and before his classes he would stare at the teenagers and young women in their tight leotards and imagine himself in the gymnasium, sweating but happy, no longer tired and drowsy. His own classes became more protracted, more tedious and unbearable.

One evening he told Stewart, 'Too much car thief in them parts. I had to drop out. Everyday, somebody from class losing they car. I don't know what this country coming to.'

'But what about the nearby police station?'

'Police. Don't tell me about police.' Stewart understood. At any rate he was happy that his regular mode of transportation would now resume every evening.

He never asked for a refund of his tuition fees.

More time was spent by Stewart's home, on the verandah listening to him talk about his plants. 'Look at those flowers on the Julie mango tree. You know what kind of flowers they is?' Stewart motioned to lilac and orange-coloured flowers growing out of some coconut husks encased in wires and suspended from the lower branches with thicker, single wires. 'Orchids. I didn't pay a cent for them. One day I was passing through Arima and I went up to Lopinot and I see them on an old immortelle tree. I cut them down the same day, the branch and everything. And then I peel off the bark.' He settled back on his chair. 'I building a fence in the back with some poui. Some of the same poui you see over there,' he said, pointing to short poui logs stuck in the ground and arranged in a semi-circle, supporting the cover of an old washing machine to shade the young plants. 'Vegetable seedlings. Afterwards, I will plant them in the back. You know,

I design this house myself,' he said suddenly. 'Do all the landscaping too.'

He thought of his own decrepit home, the sickly flowers growing in untidy clumps, overrun by weeds.

With a show of modesty Stewart said, 'But is Maria really. Is she who does be pushing me all the time. And she who have the place so spic and span.'

He told Stewart, 'This computing business does take up too much of me time. But ay-ay, I didn't tell you, I doing everything at home now. The class was just a waste of money.' He remembered the plump secretary. 'Getting fat out of poor people. And it so demanding. Sometimes I does wish for a little free time to do this and that, but I just don't have the time.'

Not too long afterwards he bought a packet of seeds and, following the instructions on the back of the packet, planted them in Styrofoam cups. For the first few days he watered the cups diligently, then seeing no progress, he stopped.

He told Stewart, 'The seeds, like they just refuse to grow.'

'Sometimes they already expire. You check the expiry date on the pack?'

Feeling ashamed, he shook his head.

'And then again, maybe you don't have the hand. If you don't have the hand, nothing will grow.'

The damn things too stiff, he thought. Can't even plant a little seed.

Then Stewart said, 'But is Maria who really have the hand, not me. Everything she plant does spring up like magic. You remember the story about the beanstalk? In no time!' After a while he said, 'Just like she sister, Clementine. She should work in the Botanic Gardens. These Spanish not easy at all. Maybe is the little bit of Carib in the two of them. Real planters,' he said with satisfaction. He picked the stem from a hibiscus plant protruding into the verandah, stripped the leaves and rotated the thicker edge into his ear. He coughed. While coughing, the words broken up into indistinct syllables, he asked, 'You ever see Clementine?'

He did not immediately understand.

'Clementine,' Stewart said, removing the stem from his ear and flicking away piece of wax. 'The wife sister. She was here just the other evening.'

He shook his head.

Well, you lucky because she here right now. Maria. Ma-a-ria.'

Maria appeared, not stepping into the verandah but peeping out and holding the curtain against her upper body to obscure the intimate home clothing that she wore.

'Where Clem?'

'Josh, go and call Auntie,' she shouted.

Like her sister, Clementine was brown, big-boned and possessed an ambiguous mixture of reserve and stridency. He thought: she is not unpleasant to look at.

One day Stewart asked him, 'You put in the extra room yet?' And he realised that it had been settled, by-passing all the formal stages. All the negotiations had taken place in his absence with Stewart filling in the details. He felt happy, thinking of the complimentary, encouraging things that might have been said: decent, hard-working, no vices, steady employment.

They were married in the Warden's Office, with Stewart as the witness. They moved into a small, downstairs apartment, rented by a family who lived upstairs. He had not bothered to explain anything to his mother: she had shown only a brief, subdued interest when he had dropped a hint about his marriage. But the days passed happily. He enjoyed the intimacy and affection that Clementine provided him. He was contented by clothes always neatly ironed, food prepared, pretty curtains deftly hung. After one visit, Stewart never returned and, strangely, never enquired about their domestic life. He, feeling ashamed of the little intimacies, never said anything.

Once he told Clementine, 'You know, if you really think about it, if you have a scale and you measuring and measuring, you could scale down these off-white people.' Her neutral, uncomprehending smile told him that she had never thought of these things. 'I like those cream colour lace curtains that you put over by the louvers. It looking nice.' She smiled more affectionately this time. His satisfaction grew. At last, he thought. At last.

But, after living in the downstairs apartment for almost four months, he found that his financial reserves, complicated by the groceries, the utilities bills, the clothes and the rent, were dwindling. He became worried. He told Stewart, 'The little egg nest finishing fast.'

It was Clementine who made the decision and he found himself anxious about the thought of returning to the house, confronting his mother rocking in her hammock. But Clementine had said, 'Isn't your mother living alone, John? We could plant up the land around the house. Two acres, isn't it?' He had nodded, frowning.

His mother's initial reaction was as bad as he had expected. The day before, in preparation, he had visited her, giving her a hundred dollar bill and explaining that he would be returning with his wife. She seemed uninterested then. But when he approached holding two over-stuffed suit cases filled with clothes, and Clementine came carrying a large plastic bag containing small decorative pieces she had brought from the apartment, he saw the energy — which he had never noticed before — seeping away from his mother's face, from her hands fallen limp in her lap, from her feet, motionless now, her heels digging into the concrete. He thought she was going to faint. 'The other things will come in the van tomorrow,' he said, nudging Clementine, bigger than him, to the stairs.

His mother, speaking through uneven gasps, said, 'I want to see how long this thing will last.' There was no need, however, for him to be worried. Clementine, in her brisk, efficient way, no sooner than they had settled, concerned herself with tidying up the house. Wallpaper was purchased to cover the holes in the wooden walls. The rotting railings were removed and steel lengths were purchased and tied with cutlass wire to the posts on the steps. Nails were bought and the creaking stopped. Strips of linoleum decorated parts of the kitchen and other square pieces served as door mats.

He told Stewart, 'The egg nest really going fast.'

Stewart smiled, his solemnity easing. 'Is always so in the beginning. But tell me, she start planting anything yet? Keep me clued in when that happen, all right?'

Then the plantings came. Stewart had exaggerated neither the enthusiasm nor the gifts of the sisters; the formerly neglected yard prospered: daisies blossomed, Sweet William bloomed, marigolds and African violets formed colourful miniature hedges. They hired a workman for a day and he instructed them about drains and soakaways, collecting the stones and broken bits of bricks himself. He went to a nearby poultry farm and returned with two bags of droppings, mixing it with garden lime, peat and clay, to form a rich planting medium. He positioned and pounded some boulders — which had been dropped by the works department to repair a depression in the road and which was never used — to form a walkway.

When the workman returned, a shed with a span roof was constructed at the side of the house for the celery, cucumber and tomato seedlings.

His mother watched from the hammock. One evening after work, he saw her looking at the seedlings, pulling out the straggly plants, compressing the loose areas. The next day he saw both of them in the makeshift greenhouse, talking about the usefulness of vegetables and trying to locate an area to plant some edible root crops such as dasheen, eddoes and cassava. He could not mask his astonishment. 'Like we will have to start selling in the market just now? With all these vegetables we growing.' They continued their discussion, paying no attention to him. But he was satisfied. And he remembered — the memory coming as a surprise to him — the time before his father's death, a time when he was just about twelve years or so, how his parents would be planting and reaping cocoa, coffee and bananas which they would later sell to a huge, terrifying-looking man named Carl Jeffrey. He remembered watching while Carl Jeffrey placed the coffee in pitch-oil tins, then into sacks, throwing the sacks in the van's tray. He recalled, too, how Mr. Jeffrey would test the bananas, squeezing the end with his fat, stained fingers until the slimy, yellow fruit popped out. Mr. Jeffrey would then swallow it with a single gulp, his moustache closing around the smothered fruit, while his father looked on impatiently. How easily he had forgotten those days when his mother, shading her eyes with a straw hat, would scatter the coffee berries and leaves on an unloosened rice bag set on the ground. He would climb up swiftly and lower another branch for her. Sometimes the scorpion ants and the bachacs, nestling between the berries, would scurry up his clothes, making him jump hastily from the tree.

Looking back, but not really certain, he felt that these might have been enjoyable days.

They grew closer, his mother and his wife: one restoring the other's passion for the land, directing her to a time of accomplishment, the other offering advice and support, happy to be useful once more.

Every day, after work, he would see them admiring the new additions to the garden or making plans for the vegetables and the yams and cassava that they expected to reap in the near future. He would study them from a distance: his wife reclining against the latticed gate at the foot of the stairs, his mother on the motionless hammock; one speaking, the other nodding, both shaking their heads and sometimes growing serious, then perhaps a half-smile on the face of one of the women, remembering some agricultural accomplishment: a bud emerging, a difficult flower surviving, a fungus kept at bay. Then one day he saw another hammock constructed at a right angle from his mother's, one post serving as the base for two ropes and another post on the left, serving as another base. They did not notice his arrival.

And that was how he found them during most evenings when he returned from work. Lying in the hammocks, swinging slowly, speaking with pride and with a secret, inclusive joy of their plants.

But their affinity excluded him.

He told Stewart, 'I thinking about signing up for the computer course again, man.'

'But what about the studies at home?'

'Where I will get the time? Planting on that side and pruning on this side. Is like the Botanic Garden in truth.'

Stewart became uncharacteristically agitated. 'It start man! It start.' He got up. You must send across some veggies for me when they bear, you hear? I just wish I had all that land like you. Maria. Ma-a-ria. You hearing that? Clem start!'

Seeing Stewart's enthusiasm, he felt sapped. 'I will send across the veggies, man. From the time they bear.'

Whenever he visited, Stewart would now ask, 'How they coming on, man? How the veggies and the flowers going?'

Unable to share Stewart's enthusiasm, the visits grew less frequent and, after a while, tapered off completely. Stewart attributed this to the new demands of married life and the inevitable obsession with plants. In the bank, Stewart would observe the unstrung, tired appearance and try to calculate how much time had been spent in the garden the evening before, how many other seedlings were planted. He would recall his own obsessive periods and then eventually the balanced, normal life he now led.

But there was no joy in this life. The joy belonged to the two women. Coming home one day and visualising the scene that he knew could confront him, he almost drove off the road when the image became perverse and he saw not two, but three hammocks, swinging side by side.

He became moody and excitable. He would tell beggars, 'Instead of begging, why you don't go and plant veggies.' He would pronounce the word as it was a disease. 'Veggies! It will feed you good, good.' The beggar would totter away. He would shout, 'Wait! Don't go. Come let me tell you how to grow you own veggies. It real easy.'

Bouts of depression seized him. He became sullen and withdrawn, hardly speaking to the bank's employees, not mentioning the computers again. He started drinking, entering the rum shop nervously and feeling like an intruder and then, after forcing the first beer down his throat, feeling more relaxed, attempting conversations with fellow drinkers, becoming more drunk, for a while freed from his troubles and speaking with an elaborate ease. In a short time, he gained a reputation in the bars. The other customers, observing his well-dressed appearance and his initial reserve, felt that he was either a teacher or some important civil servant who had broken away from the system, easing, in this place, the demands of his suffocating profession.

'What going on, Teach? What you think of all this strike and lock-out that we reading about these days?'

And they would observe his response, hearing not so much the words, but rather, would notice how he inclined his head, how the hands, stiff and authoritative, would come down on the table in disgust or with barely controlled cynicism, sometimes cleaving through the air in an arc, emphasising some point.

But the drinking did not agree with him. He would awaken about three or four in the morning, his throat dry, his head throbbing. Hurrying for a drink of water, sometimes gargling by the stairs, he would be struck with guilt, wondering whether he had said anything in his drunkenness to indicate he was not a teacher, but a lowly worker in the bank. Back on the bed, his wife would place her hands affectionately on his chest, enquiring whether anything was wrong. 'Nothing,' he would mumble, feeling the hand heavy on his body. 'Nothing. Go back and sleep.' The rest he would say silently. You have plenty planting to do tomorrow. The veggies need you. The two of you.

He began staring more intently at the rosy-cheeked girl in the bank, looking for any flicker of interest, any sign of encouragement. Later, he would fantasise. Images of her as a doomed maiden swirled around in his head. Kidnapped by lecherous accountants. In urgent need of a blood transfusion. Her home suddenly re-possessed and she with nowhere to go. And always he would enter the images, rescuing her, offering his blood, offering his home.

One day, while giving her a folder, he squeezed her finger suddenly and violently. She withdrew her hand swiftly, giving him a look of such withering hatred that he knew that the fantasies would be forever tarnished, viable no longer.

He improvised. During the days, in the bank, he carried out his duties in a sullen, withdrawn manner and with a constant sense of his diminishing importance, while at nights, with his wife's hand heavy on his chest, he would become a man of extraordinary abilities. He would imagine then, while lying on the bed, startling a group of accountants and computer programmers by throwing a glass into the air and holding it there by the force of his amazing will-power. Sometimes he would walk through thick concrete walls or materialise things. But the fantasies were always defective. The glass would come crashing to the floor; the concrete walls would harden, enclosing and trapping him forever; he would materialise obscene, disgusting things.

He began to spend most of his weekends at the seaside, remote, hidden areas where no one visited. There he would look for fossils, examining the loosened rocks, prying out small layers of shale. He would think of the hidden remains of long-lost cities and of dinosaur bones. Just before dusk, at the time of the mellowing of the day, he would remember a poem from his primary school days and would, briefly, see himself as an Arawak, living his comfortable life, wandering naked on the beaches. And then Columbus' doom-laden ships would appear, bearing down on him.

One night on his way home, a car had followed him along a deserted stretch for more than half-an-hour. He never returned to the beach.

The nights passed slowly; the days became intolerable. When his wife became pregnant he was suffused with feelings of guilt and of panic. He would awaken with the guilt and in the lavatory and afterwards, washing himself, a feeling of sustained helplessness would overwhelm him. His mother moved into the room and at nights, sleeping now in her old hard bed, with the protruding ends of the coconut fibre stinging his back, he would hear both women speaking in low voices. He would hear the springs creaking while his mother massaged his wife and would feel even more apprehension when he realised that the sounds he thought were so intimate could be carried out of the room. It had never really been a private place.

In the morning he would examine the welts caused by the coconut fibres and the mosquito bumps and experience a sense of dreadful certainty that he had contracted some horrible disease. He would rub the bumps and welts until the areas became reddened and inflamed. Applying some burning astringent lotion to the affected areas, he would sometimes place the cotton balls in his ears, listening to the muffled sounds. Sometimes he would place the cotton into his nostrils, attempting to breathe through the soft, furry, ball. When it became lodged deep inside his nostril he would hurriedly pluck out the cotton ball with a pair of tweezers, staring at the moist, round ball. He would then taste it, rolling it about on his tongue. Realising what he had done he would scream in a frightened rage.

One morning, lying in bed, he listened to his wife vomiting in the face basin, hearing the sound through the cracks in the wall. He arose in a rage, advancing towards the wall. He began to cough, and the rage turned instead on his coughing. As the hacking increased and his thin chest heaved and vibrated, he thought: Oh God, like I too catch the damn romki now. When the coughing subsided, he put his face by a large crack in the wall and shouted, 'Nobody don't worry. Only donkey does catch romki. Listen to how fine the wheezing is. Not coarse at all.' He emitted a dry, grunting wheeze and ended up in another fit of coughing.

He heard his wife saying, 'John, that cough sounding bad. You should use something.'

His voice sounded brittle, 'You right. Just see if you could spray anything through this crack right here and I will keep me mouth open on the other side and collect it with me tongue.'

He waited. 'What happen, you didn't find the spray yet? Hurry up girl, me mouth beginning to pain.' He heard the slow, heavy footsteps of his mother and then the sound of paper being crumpled and thrust and fitted into the crack. He probed with his finger; tying to dislodge the paper. When the tiny splinters began to graze his finger, he stopped. And cursed. But knowing that his mother was on the other side of the wall, he lowered his voice.

He went back to his bed and observed the number of disengaged hairs scattered on the pillow. He saw a mosquito camouflaged within the curly hairs and brought his hand down savagely. He plucked off the wings and legs, one by one, then placed the insect on the table, watching its helpless movements. He saw the bloated abdomen and violently brought his hands down, destroying the mosquito. 'That is my blood you so full up with, you little bitch. Every blasted body here want to suck me out now.'

In the other room his wife, her voice distorted by the running water enquired, 'What's the matter, John?'

And like a rusty, grating echo, his mother asked, 'What happen to him now. What he mashing up so?'

He considered the mangled remains of the insect on the table.

The vomiting came again.

The spot of blood in his palm began to tingle, then irritate him. He placed his palm by his nose, attempting to smell the scent of the soap, but all he got was the rancid odour of his unwashed mouth.

His mother, somewhere in the kitchen now, asked, 'What happen, he didn't get up yet?' After a while she said, loudly enough for him to hear, 'This condition you in, and youself have to go to the market. Trouble and more trouble. Lord!' She stretched the last word, so that it sounded like a groan.

He made a funnel with his hands and directed the odour from his mouth directly into his nostrils. He inhaled deeply. The door was slammed shut and the footsteps — heavy and dragging, sounded on the stairway. Peering through the curtain and watching the two women walking down the road, he tried to imagine their conversation. He narrowed his eyelids and became alarmed when the illusion of multiple mothers and wives was created. Quickly, he adjusted his vision and instead focused unflinchingly on the area between both women, until the two figures grew closer; then merged. He smiled; it was easier to concentrate his hatred on one entity. He squinted until he could see them no longer, then cast his gaze downwards, to the greenhouse just under the window. The cabbage and cauliflower stalks swayed gracefully within the little fluttering bursts of breeze. He coughed and vibrated his throat, searching for phlegm, then spat a round, yellowish ball at the seedling bed. The ball fell short. He hawked desperately and spat but once more the ball fell short. The cabbage and cauliflower danced and cavorted with the breeze.

When he rushed downstairs, and in spite of the boiling anger that encased him, he was careful to hold on to the railings and to calculate his steps. He remembered his mother saying, just before they had left, 'You pregnant and he take maternity leave. Lord, help me please'. The thoughts came swiftly, flooding his mind and clouding his intent, so that he barely knew what he was doing. He thought: so I take maternity leave. So I pregnant now. Why they don't ring up *The Enquirer* then. Pregnant man found in Trinidad. No, better if we start up the story like this. Women rocking in hammock suddenly discover pregnant man in vicinity. Women screamed and fainted. Man continued walking.

The cabbage and cauliflower danced before him. He brought his thumb and forefinger together and neatly clipped off one of the stalks. 'Snip. Locust'. A bud fell on the bed. 'Snip. Grasshopper'. Another fell. His hand moved like scissors through the bed. Then he remembered the two women speaking with expertise and confidence about the various pests that they had to be on the alert for. 'Don't frighten mealy-bug and aphid. All you turn coming. Snip everybody.' Within the incoherent rage, a sobering thought appeared. What kind of a damn stupid name for a insect is mealy-bug? The rage briefly quickened, and then, just as fast, fell away. The nursery bed looked like it had been recently mowed; the headless stalks stood clumsy and immobile.

At about 11.30 a.m. that morning, he shifted unto his belly, scratched his bottom three times and fell into a troubled sleep. He awoke after a few minutes and, for the first time, considered the profound futility of boredom. And then, at that very instant, he knew what had to be done.

His mind became ordered, each fresh thought chasing away some of the lethargy that had taken hold of him. He thought: no rope, no soft candle, nothing sharp, nothing cutting. Like a chemist, he set about his task. Quarter glass of dishwashing detergent. His brain worked quickly. Add a little dash of Aldrex and some nailpolish remover to liven up the mixture. He stirred. The potion looked soapy and harmless. He dropped two blocks of ice into the glass. Then he got out his pen and paper and began to write:

To those concerned,

This is just a little note to anybody who may care to read it. Bury me or better still plant me next to the dasheen and yam so that I will be able to get the best of care. And if, by chance, I get fertilise regular, I could grow into a nice, strong tree that everybody could swing they hammock from.

Sometimes I feel that I causing too much trouble and that I am of no use. Or rather, I should state that nobody appreciate my real value because they unable to see that I could be a great man, if only I could get the chance. But nobody want to give me that chance. That is why I feel that I should move on. Move on to a more happy place. So if anybody see a little light twinkling up in the sky, don't be afraid, that will just be your humble servant, John, looking down on everybody. Sometimes, in the dry season, I will fly between the clouds and try to encourage a little rain for the veggies.

I remain,
John Fitzgerald Tennyson,
Son and Husband
(No longer now).

PS. You could put these last three lines on my gravestone.

He placed the paper into his pocket, already formulating the next stage. The windows were slammed shut, the doors closed. While sipping the mixture, he caught a whiff of the gas oozing out of the stove. He went to his bed and, for the third time that day, attempted to drift into some form of unconsciousness. A strange smile layered itself across his face. So easy, he thought. The end of planting, the end of his exclusion, the end of everything. Just before he dozed off, the smile, partly through lack of practice, curved downwards and converted itself into a scowl. This was the expression they found him with.

With half-closed eyelids, he saw the blurred image of his wife opening the window and fanning herself with an old McDonald's Almanac. Then he heard his mother's voice. 'Lord almighty! You mean to say he couldn't turn off the gas before he went to sleep.'

He heard windows being opened in anger and haste.

'He was maybe a little tired,' his wife said, not, he noted, as an apology; but rather as a statement designed to produce a fresh burst of irritation from his mother.

'You right. Is a hard job sleeping whole day. He must be overtired.'

He felt the need to do something drastic, something overpowering in its destruction but another urge quickly took hold of him. The upheavals in his stomach came without warning. 'Woman, move you tail from in front me,' he said to no one in particular, as he rushed to the lavatory. The diarrhoea lasted for two hours and, seated on the bowl, he felt the dehydration spreading throughout his body. He felt limp and shrivelled and he peered downwards curiously. In that position, with the blood rushing to his head, he barely heard his mother quarrelling about the seedlings.

The suicide had been a terrible failure.

Two months after his release from the St. Ann's Mental Institution, he was paid a visit by Stewart. When he saw the stocky figure, fidgeting, the feet tapping nervously, he felt an odd moment of tenderness. He knew that Stewart did not want to come, but now that he was here, was thinking of something comforting and helpful to say.

Stewart asked, 'So how the veggies doing, man. And the baby too? How they doing?'

He placed his foot on the concrete and steadied the hammock. 'They coming along. They coming along.' He could think of nothing more to say.

After a moment of silence, Stewart said uneasily, 'They have this new fella in the bank now man. Young little boy. New out of college. We does get along so-so. But he green man. Real green under the skin.'

John Fitzgerald Tennyson accepted the compliment. His yellowish teeth showed.

Footsteps sounded on the stairway. 'The two planters', Stewart said, as he saw Maria and Clementine.

'And look, planter number three', John Fitzgerald Tennyson whispered, looking at his mother coming down the steps.

'John, just hold Hazel here for a minute. I going to show Maria the flowers garden.'

He inclined his head up from the hammock and tenderly took the baby. 'Make sure to show she the grape vine that I plant, eh', he shouted at the departing women. Resting back his head on the hammock, he placed the baby gently on his chest. He smelt the baby powder and the soft, fresh baby odour and closed his eyes. The hammock creaked.

Just when Stewart thought he must have dozed off, he heard, 'I thinking about taking up preaching. All them visions I had up in St. Ann's, I have to put to good use.'

Then the creakings sounded again. The baby gurgled. John Fitzgerald Tennyson purred softly, tickling the baby's chin. 'I have to put up a small baby hammock soon,' he said, smiling.

HEADING FOR THE COLD

The way I see it, a country with a stupid shape like this one can't have too much smart people in it. The place make up like one of them brown paper bag that you blow up with air and ring up the four side, and sometime I does wish that this was really the case because I woulda bring me hand together and badam! Mash up the damn place and kill all the kiss-me-ass bitches in it. Any side you tu'n is only smartmen, vagrant and politician you seeing, and I personally feel that the last set is the wo'st because, once every five years when is election time, you seeing them springing up all over the place like knot-grass, opening standpipe and latrin' and cutting ribbon left, right and centre. Any time you see one of them with a scissors in he back pocket, you could bet election round the corner. But I not complaining, because that is the only time a lil work does take place and a lil money does pass, although the other day one of the minister fella was real lucky. He had was to visit this refinery, and two days before they painting up all the tank and ole iron where he was suppose to pass — listen to me carefully, eh, I say painting over, not repairing — just before he reach near this place where it have something called a cat-cracker — don't ask me what kinda name is that — anyways, as I was saying, near the cat-cracker one big explosion take place. Nobody get damage in that one, but I hear that the minister lock he door and didn't come out from he house for days afterwards. Me, I not crying for nobody. Who get blow up, get blow up; who dead, well dead. I have me own worries to study.

People does feel that driving maxi-taxi is easy wo'k and that most of we is just rapist looking out for little school children to moless, but you see me, I not in that kinda stupidness. In the fuss place I can't take on this younger generation who does just jump in me maxi as if they own it and say, 'Driver, run some good music for we'. I tell you, for hours afterwards, when I in the bathroom or when I in the bed with Sybil, that thing does be ringing in me ears. I remember long time when I was driving taxi for a Indian fella name Palloo, I only uses to have nice music by James Brown and Kitch and Sparrow and everybody in the car happy like pappy. Now them little hen and them, with they hair pile up high-high on the top, and wearing earring and fancy chain, only quarrelling for that Jamaican stupidness. Sometimes I does feel that I should take the gilpin I does keep below me seat in case anybody give me a bad drive, and planass each and every one. 'You they, come here, two planass for wearing that stupid earring'. 'Across here, step forward, three planass for that dotish haircomb'. And the school-girls in the back, one planass each for giggling and carrying on like apprentice bats!' Ah well, that is the thing that does be going on in me head even though I know that I can't do nobody nothing.

That is why I want to leave this place.

For a good few years I planning this move. I done tell Sybil that one day I will just ups and sell the maxi and pay off the bank and dust it to the cold. She, poor thing, does just shake she head and say, 'Anything you say, Reuben.' I feel she don't take me on serious, but one day she will get the shock of she life when I just pack up, lock, stock and barrel. When I say I heading for the cold, I not talking about no refugee nonsense either eh, I more interested in this thing one of me passengers was telling me about. Just pass two thousand, he say, and you getting all you papers and particulars backdated in some form over they as if you was living they for a long, long time, and then all you have to do is apply for this thing they call amnesty. I does know that, as how I black and not so educated, I will have one or two ups and downs in the beginning, but over here not much better, don't mind what all of them big boys does be talking about rainbow country. They way I see it, rainbow does only come up after rain, but it look like rain tu'ning to storm and hurricane before this rainbow they mouthing off about going to crop up.

Don't just take my word for it, but in this business I does hear all kinda things. Just the other day two people board me maxi. One was a fat-belly Indian, the kind they does call F.B.I., and the other one was a ole Creole with he hair like a flannel ball and looking like if he pass through a good few world wars. I can't say how the argument begin, but all of a sudden I hear the old Creole telling the fat Indian man that all Indian people interested in is t'iefing poor people money. He say the whole pack of them is t'iefing and conniving scamps. Well the Indian fella, he mouth smelling of white rum, say that these days every time he open the papers, is some Creole discover that Moses was a creole, Jesus was a creole, everybody was a creole. He say that the creole race just hijacking all these top class people like if long time is only one setta people they had living. Well, I just listening quiet quiet, waiting for the fight to break out, but the best joke is that after they drop out, I see the two of them head across by the bar opposite the maxi-taxi stand and sit down on two stool, sipping they rum cool cool, like ole time pally-wallies.

Me. I keeping out of this racial talk. Black as I is — even though me hair more wavy than curly — I keeping me distance.

I done hear that people say that one day over here will get like Guyana and I hope that by the time that happen I done up in the colder region.

Just imagine the ole Reuben sitting down in one of them plastic chairs they does have by the swimming pool and sipping the sorta drink that have orange slice and these little round fruits, and chatting with Joan Collins and Raquel Welch. But I must keep me mout' shut and keep all these things to meself because I realise that Sybil can't take a little joke. Swelling up like a ole bull-frog and then saying, 'When you will get time to sit down and sip you fancy drink and chat with Joan Collins? After you clean out the pool and sweep up the hotel?' Leave she. She go lorn the hard way.

I not saying that when I reach I not going to put down a little hard wo'k first, eh. Understand that. From the way I hear it, everybody does have it on the rough side in the beginning, but to tell you personally, not me and that cleaning out toilet and cesspit business at all, sah. Not at all. That part I really can't take on. Gimme lawn to mow or window to wash or gas-station thing. All that okay, but not no toilet and cesspit business for me. I hear big big people in this place just retire from they air-condition office and fling down in the cold and doing that kinda stupidness. That is the part I does can't understand. Them sorta people have no right to end up so and sometimes I does feel is just vice in they head.

Vice! Any side you tu'n! Just a month aback this vagrant fella slip in me maxi and piss down all over me back seat and then step out back again. Cool-cool. Like if is he own personal urinal or something. If I did bounce him up doing that nastiness, well, I woulda make a jail in truth, because I woulda slice out he business first of all and then rumfle him up good and proper with me gilpin. I really don't know what this place coming to nah. Is seventeen years I driving taxi, North-South, S'ando, Curepe — Chaguanas, all down Rio and Princes Town side and I never yet bounce up stupidness so. Is like people in this place all of a sudden start to take in so. It look like now money finish, sense finish too. People go surprise to hear the kinda talk I does hear in this line o' wo'k. Like, for instance this lady, black and greasy like if she just slip down from a ham-pole, saying that she want to move up to Valsayn because she can't stand mingling with too much black people all the time, or like these Indian schoolgirl — with no bag, I just remember that — talking 'bout this newtime popular bat who does be singing and carrying on like Marilyn Monroe. Guess what was they ambition? If you say to come out like the bat, you damn right. Me? I different. When I talking 'bout the cold, is a different scene I in, not this high-falutin kinda attitude.

Now, I don't like people to get the idea that I complaining, eh, but the thing is, in this business you does know what going on in the whole blasted country. Who outsmarting who. Who take away who husband. Who taking drugs. People look like they does just wait to jump in Reuben maxi before they start minding other people business, and the old Reuben too, he not easy eh, because this ears here like a funnel, and the whole day it just absorbing information. To tell you the truth, I feel that one day I must write a book. I not joking. Really, really write a book. People go laugh, but who know this place better than me? And the next thing is that in this book — I feel that I go call it 'From Reuben Pen', that sounding nice — anyways, in this book I not mincing matters. I calling a spade a spade, and I giving Jack he jacket. I exposing up all them big-shot who does walk about pointing they snout up in the air like if they scorn everybody else, forgetting they come out from someway behind God back. All the priest and religious people who eyeing, first of all money and, second of all, women. All them teachers who does walk in the classroom with a nip of rum stock up they back-pocket and all them police who in more bobol and skulduggery than anybody else. You understand where I coming from? Reuben have the goods on plenty people in this place. And not that alone, because all the years I hustling up and down the place, I know it like the back of me hand. I could describe Por' -Spain like a book with one half nice and pretty, and all the lawn mow up real nice, and the next half like a courbeaux town with rubbish and cardboard house and half-naked children peeping out. All down Rio side with pot-hole and land-slip left, right and centre, and drivers dadging about and cussing the wind. And the night time, don't talk about that. I does be listening to them good with they vampirey behaviour. In the night, everybody have some big plan or fancy idea. How to do this, how to do that. How to make money How to get lazy people to work. How to set the country going. I does listen to them careful but the best joke is, in the daytime these same people travelling in me maxi like half-dead po-me-one with they mouth open and they eye close, and not saying a single wo'd. Like how people does wear two-tone shoes, this place like it have two-tone people. Nice eh? From Reuben pen. That book going to be a real best-sella, man. When I finish, I know plenty people go vex but, like the old deafie uses to say, 'Who don't like it could go to hell'.

That remind me of some of them new time top-boys we have now, who pretending that they is high class world leaders, because if it have a war a million miles away, they popping up on T.V. saying that they displease. Them displease! Anything happen in Russia or America, you seeing them staring down at you from the T.V. mouthing off and prattling and carrying on like little gujay-rat that lose they hole. Don't ask me if anybody does take them on, I don't know, but I could tell you that while they trying to play emperor and pope, people down here more interested in who going to get lay-off, who going to get highjack on the highway next, who going to get a loan to buy school books, and thing like that. But I feel that in me book I going to leave them politician fellas one side. I don't want to mix up in that business too much because, as far as I concern, all of them is the same damn thing. Sometimes I does feel that we should get these lie detector kinda gadgets they does have in the cold and well test them up, but they go blow out all the kiss-me-ass fuse in the electricity company. Excuse me language, but that is the very exact reason why I keeping them outa this book, because this time Reuben go really make a jail, and, to tell you the truth, I not design for no cell or prison because I does even feel real cramp-up coming from Por'-Spain before I hit the highway jam morning and evening and you partner sweating in the maxi and cussing all the passengers in he mind.

That is why I does step down sometimes to Valencia or Caura River with a few of the boys. We done plan a lime this Sunday evening and bald-head Tankoo promise to bring half a shark and two carite. The way I thinking about that fish broff, with the season fish and the cooking fig and yam, and dumpling thicker than Sybil tongue, steaming below the 'mortelle tree by the river bank, me mout' watering already. Is like this. After I put down about two plateful, and a lil' white rum in me head, I does hit the cool river water and sometimes I does float on me back and watch how the sun looking like a jigsaw puzzle behind all the bamboo and the 'mortelle flowers floating down like small orange colour bell, and all the worries does drift away from me mind.

Not too bad, eh? That is the way I want to live when I more ageable. Don't get me wrong eh, I didn't forget about going to the cold. All that in the back of me head, but in the meantime, the old Reuben go tough it out and try to bypass all them bigboys gimmick and promise and ole talk, and cool heself down by the river with pot bubbling and the water lapping against he back.

DESIGNS

Charles Parmassar settled down in his swivel chair, placed his feet against the rusty metal table and rocked back. Closing his eyes, he saw himself somewhere in the past, before the departure of his wife and children. He probed these memories for moments of joy and ease and encountered only emptiness. He shifted his focus and saw himself inert and powerless, seated on the swivel chair. He opened his eyes and felt that the inner vision was real. When his hand passed over his face, he felt all the imperfections: the soft, weak skin swelling just beneath the eyes, a pulpy nose that indicated neither strength nor weakness and a lower lip which, in moments of solitude, would grow slack.

'Mr Parmassar.' Quickly the lip snapped back. He realised that he had been caressing it and that his fingers were wet. He wiped his fingers over his oiled hair.

'Yes?' He surveyed her. He saw that she was wearing a red dress that matched the red blotches on her face and hands. He looked towards her legs. She frowned.

'I come for the plans,' she said. 'You finish it? Is almost six weeks now. You say that it will take four.'

Four, five, six. What's the difference, he thought, for a man who has to spend all his time designing houses. He remembered her and her newly acquired husband crowding his little office with their vulgar dreams, offering their inane ideas and impractical suggestions. He hated these newly married couples who came to him so bloated with confidence and hope, expecting him to accommodate all their wretched emotions in his design.

The scene fixed in his mind. She had wanted a space in the hallway for her Italian Regency mirror. The husband had smiled. She wanted a large, spacious living room. The husband had bent closer, savouring all her suggestions. After a while the woman had grown less precise about what she wanted and had begun to boast about the glazed green ceramic tiles she had already purchased, about the ceiling fan, the brass finish beanpot lamp and the calligraphy box made somewhere in Korea.

Now she stood before him with a declamatory look.

'Come back in one week time,' he said. 'I still have some patching up to do.'

'Patching up?' she asked suspiciously.

'Just some fine details,' he said.

After she had left, her accusations hovered around the room. He levered himself out of his chair, cursing his arthritic joints and opened the window. As his gaze flickered over the dusty shelves, the unplastered hollow-clay block walls without any proper ventilation, the irony of his situation was not lost on him.

Edmund Parmassar, architect of over thirty years' experience, designer of houses for bankers, civil servants and business men, secreted inside this tiny cell.

Ah, but no time for that now. His fingers shuddered with anticipation as he opened the drawer and withdrew the grey, waxy, paper, folded neatly three times. His palms slid over the paper, feeling the texture of the walls he had designed, passed lightly over the small kitchen, lingered by the bedroom that was so apart from the rest of the house. Then they rested on the room which she had wanted for visitors.

This was Pauline's house. She was different. With her, there was no counterfeit blitheness, no unnecessary exhibition of happily married bliss. She had not hinted at a husband or an impending marriage. She was so different from the other stained, blemished woman.

And it was she who promised to bring to fruition what he had long envisaged but could never accomplish. He remembered the faint smile barely twisting the corners of her lips, holding there for a moment as if assessing whether to burst out into laughter or to retain its privacy.

Before her, his desire had seemed like a perversion, acts to be ashamed of. There were the late night visits to the houses that he had created, had known so intimately, seeing the dim, distorted lights through the bedroom curtain, and through another window; a brief glow, the refrigerator being opened, calculating the distance from the kitchen to the stairway and trying to construct what had happened, what was happening. There was the intense scrutiny of the copies of the plans that he kept in his drawer, trying to create incidents from the architecture that he had designed, assessing the state of the occupants' lives, wondering about the little quarrels that sprang up between the dining room and the verandah, about the sudden brief moments of tenderness in the bedroom, the secrets kept behind closed doors.

But it was useless; the doors remained closed and the lives remained remote. Even in the streets, a casual encounter revealed no secrets, told no story.

'So how the house going?' he would ask.

Invariably the answer would be, 'It holding out. A few cracks appearing here and there but otherwise...'

That day in the office Paula was demure one minute, insistent the next, and with none of the phoney capriciousness that typified much of his clientele.

'I would like to build a house,' she had said.

At first he was surprised. He tried to match her smile. There was something fluid about everything she did, each motion retaining a vestige of some earlier action.

'So what style you thinking about: split-level, flat, posts?'

She considered. 'It's the inside that interests me. You may...' she hesitated, '...just design any ol' outside for me. I just have some vague ideas.'

But her ideas were not vague and as Edmund Parmassar drew the rough sketches in his notebook and as she peered over the notebook he found himself studying her clothing, the little rolling motions of her hands, her features. At first he thought that she might have been an Indian woman, but in her buoyant smile, the arching of the eyebrows, and the brief, disconcerting expression in the eyes, he saw the vestiges of other races. She withdrew a cigarette from a pack in her purse and held it between her fingers.'

'Where you get all these ideas from?' he asked.

'Oh, from here and there. I've travelled.'

Travelled.

Her potential grew.

'And you come back here, to live in this place? We go have to put in plenty burglar-proofing then.' He realised with surprise that he was speaking in dialect. There is no need, he reassured himself. Words are just words. His own casualness startled him.

'Nah. No burglar-proofing. I want to be free.'

She lit the cigarette and inhaled strenuously. He waited for the exhalation. When it came the smoke emerged in a straight line towards him, dissipating just before his chest and floating upwards. 'You is a expert smoker,' he said. She did not answer but inclined her head upwards and exhaled another thin shaft of smoke. He watched the smoke curling towards the ceiling, and then looked at her, at the head tilted upwards and felt that the momentary retention of the pose was intended to hold some significance.

'Ever been in love?' she asked.

There was no provocation; she said it like a simple statement but he could not find an answer. She laughed, then bringing her gaze downward, her eyes barely passing his, she said, 'Architecture is like painting and music you know. There must be emotion in every detail.'

When she had left, the image that lingered was not her question about love but of the smoke slipping between her lips like subdued gasps, claiming his face, his chest, his body.

His hand hovered above the telephone, hesitated, then dropped back on the tracing paper. Everything in the room, all his drafting implements seemed magnified and alive. The scissors, masking tape, aerosol spray, adhesives and arrowmounts seemed to be moving. He squinted. Was the T-square simply dangling in the air, or was it shifting closer to the drawing stand. But when he finally spoke to her, his voice was weary and sounded like another person's. He realised too late that he could find no precise reason for wanting to meet her. 'Just some patching up,' he managed to stutter. But the design had already been submitted to the Town and Country Board for approval, and when he realised that she must know that, he wondered why she had been so accommodating.

The thought helped him.

That Tuesday morning, dark clouds floated listlessly, searching for mooring. Inside the shuttered annex Edmund Parmassar felt at peace. As he awaited the coming turbulence, the stray drops falling lightly on the galvanised roof, then the brief respite before huge bucketfuls of water tumbled down, muffling the initial burst of thunder, he felt his emotions reined in, estranged from all this wasteful energy.

A drop of water suspended from the ceiling, gathered form and plunged, bursting on an instrument shelf. He thought of a translucent tadpole. Another drop took shape. He counted. When he reached forty-seven — feeling that each drop represented a year of his life — she walked in.

'Gosh all that rain,' she said as she settled on the chair, rearranging her skirt and allowing him a glimpse of her creamed, glistening knees. Then she turned away slightly and, as if speaking to the shuttered louvres, asked, 'So?'

Outside the rain came in bursts. Inside, another tadpole was forming. 'If this continue so, in a little while, the whole of Port-of-Spain will be under flood,' he said.

'Just like Atlantis,' she said, stretching the last word. 'Anyways,' she made a small movement which redefined her posture, 'what's the problem? The plans have already been submitted, haven't they.'

'Yes, I know, but I have some contacts,' he said, surprised at the swiftness of the lie.

'You mean...' she gave a small sigh. 'Nothing really change, eh?'

'How you mean? Look at all the new fancy building...'

'I mean the people,' she said. 'Everyone wants something. Everyone trying to cut a deal. And nobody coming out in the open.'

He felt his lower lip slipping downwards. 'You want the louvres open slightly? It so stuffy in here.'

'I'll do it,' she said, rising out of her chair. She reached upwards for the lever, her skirt rising against her thigh. She retained this position as if stretching her muscles, then turned around very suddenly, too suddenly for Edmund Parmassar to mask the focus of his scrutiny.

'Is this better now?' she asked, smiling, with the lips pressed tightly against each other, the cheeks filling out and giving her face an almost triangular shape.

'All architects should design something like you.' He heard his voice straining against the drifting beat of the rain.

'What?' She laughed, the sound ringing within the room. 'What made you say that?' The laughter was still in her voice but accompanied now by an insistent curiosity. A small breeze forced through the opened louvres and brought some of her smell to him, aromatic and inviting.

Accessible. The word came to him. He relaxed. 'All architects admire beautiful structures. That is our job.'

She inclined her head, offering him once more her profile. 'I remember what you said about creators putting emotions in their works.'

She lit a cigarette, the smoke forming a fine, diaphanous circle.

'That is my problem,' he continued. 'I put too much emotion into my work.' She remained silent, playing with the smoke. 'You see, I always wondering about what happening in the buildings that I design. Is like if I leave a little camera and it recording everything that take place. All the argument and the bacchanal and the patching-up and love-making. Everything. I feel sometimes like if a part of the house belong to me or maybe a part of me remain in the house and that I have a right to know.' He looked at her face through the web of smoke. 'But off and on I feel like a spy peeping though a keyhole or hiding under the couch or the bed. I don't know if is a deeper interest in the work I create, if is simple curiosity or if is just some dirty perversion. But that is the way I live my life now.'

The words came unsought, his voice dry and distant. The smoke floating in the small room tickled his throat. The rain lessened. He thought: Why am I telling her this? She was staring through the opened louvres, her expression softening. He thought of the blood rippling beneath her skin and felt that he had made contact with some part of her which had been offered, whether openly or teasingly he did not know. 'I'm sorry for burdening you with all these stupid things,' he said in a low voice.

'I have to go now,' she said, resting her fingers on his hand.

But she held back, did not look at him, her head tilted slightly, her eyes probing the corners of the cluttered office.

The lights flickered, a power failure caused by the thunder shower. Feeling the strength of her fingers, he detached himself briefly, saw the merest hint of surprise, then said, 'Just one minute.' He returned to the office, retrieved the waxy tracing paper he had been staring at prior to her visit, folded it neatly and placed it in the pocket of his trousers.

Outside, she was looking at the flickering light through the opened door. He turned off the power.

THE OCCASIONAL SADHU

He was in a drugstore; the type that sold senna, lamp-oil, soft candle, fresh aloe leaves and a variety of laxatives and skin creams made from the local weeds that grew wild in every backyard, but in the drugstore were dried, ground and packed loosely in cylindrical bottles about three inches long.

The owner of the drugstore, a man of about forty, but looking much older, appeared flustered and impatient. He had squinting eyes and a furrowed face from counting and re-counting all the dollar bills and coins before placing them in a cellophane bag, not inside the cash register, but in a drawer beneath the counter. That was more than ten years ago but I can still remember his sudden burst of anger.

'Get out! Get out! Look how you driving away all the customers!' Desperation seeped into the anger. He seemed to be helping the man out but I remember the final shove that propelled him out of the door.

The owner turned to my grandfather, who had come to buy some medication for his high blood pressure, 'I don't know what this place coming to. Every side is vagrant and beggar trying to get what little money you have.'

Through the glass door, I saw the man holding some coins

uselessly with one hand and balancing on the lamp-post with the other. Then he moved off, limping awkwardly.

Later, on our way to the taxi-stand, past the stores selling footwear, agricultural implements, old brown magazines and religious pictures, past piles of rubbish and bottles, we saw him sitting on an old piece of cardboard, just next to an old woman who looked on with detached hostility as we approached.

My grandfather, overweight and unable or unwilling to sit, stood over him, and I, about fifteen or so, looked on. He appeared to recognise us from the drug-store. I recall thinking that he looked embarrassed and wanted then to tell him that I had seen the money in his hand.

My grandfather held out a green, five dollar note. It seemed so simple: like the termination of some business transaction.

The face, brown with streaks of grey beard, remained impassive, then the eyes softened, seeming to acknowledge the act. He shook his head. My grandfather held the money, made a sound as if clearing his throat, then replaced the bill in his shirt pocket.

The man went into the taxi with us. I cannot remember what exactly was said to him but I recall that when the car slowed by the traffic-light, he, perhaps thinking that this unusual act of benevolence had run its course, opened the door and placed his guava-wood walking stick on the asphalt road. My grandfather, with the merest wisp of amusement, said, 'Wait, wait. We ain't reach yet.' For the entire journey he remained silent, and with the wind blowing his long, greyish hair backwards, I thought how much he looked like those swamis and yogis that my grandfather had often told me stories about, adding his fanciful touch and endowing them with powers and virtues beyond ordinary humans. But when I observed the torn, chequered shirt and the frayed khaki trousers, the image seemed discordant and almost blasphemous.

When we arrived, he stood at the entrance to the tent, clutching his small, brown leatherette pouch, the type used by taxi-drivers to keep their money, driving permits and insurance certificates. My grandfather was speaking to my parents and a few of the villagers who had assisted during the last few days. He was a sadhu, my grandfather was saying, and would stay with us for the next seven days.

At that time we were holding a Ramayan Yagna. This ran for seven nights of storytelling, singing and chanting and then finally, the feeding. Visitors listened, ate, and left. A few, however, seemed moved; they remained after the feeding. During the preparations, I remember thinking what a waste it all was. Bamboo sliced and patterned into elaborate canopies; yards and yards of crepe paper cut and fashioned into intricate designs; religious pictures hurriedly purchased, others crudely drawn by the village artists; knocking, hammering, tying, fastening, hanging: unending noise and activity. I wondered why all this was not held in the temple just a mile away. But my father explained that my grandparents wanted it to be held at their home before they died and I recall being satisfied with the explanation.

My grandfather was saying, 'He will sleep with the other sadhus and them in the corner of the stage.'

My mother seemed worried. 'What kinda sadhu he is, wearing them clothes?'

'Is okay. We will get a dhoti and a merino for him,' my father said.

A simple matter: a change of clothes transforming him, in my mother's eyes, from being a useless vagrant to someone pious and holy. It was the type of uncomplicated ritualism she lived by. And that night, huddling with the other sadhus, he really looked the part. The following morning I was awakened by the voice of one of my uncles.

'Aye man. What you doing they?'

I roused myself and went to the gallery.

My uncle was still shouting, 'Aye, take care you fall down. Leave all that alone.'

I peered down. The man was hobbling about collecting the pieces of paper on which the prasad was served and putting them into an empty ricebag. He seemed not to hear, collecting the paper, straightening the chairs, resting against the bamboo post to catch his breath, then limping off again. When he reached the stage on which the other sadhus were still sleeping, he sat and wiped his forehead.

My grandfather said, 'A cripple doing all this while them lazy vagabond and them still sleeping.'

I was surprised. I had never heard him refer to the sadhus in this manner.

When my father went for the ricebag, he waved him away.

This was the pattern for the next few days. During the night he would sit in the corner of the stage next to the temporary bamboo wall, listening to the discourses and the singing, and the following morning he would awaken before anyone else, cleaning, fixing and rearranging. Once or twice my father asked him to stop, explaining that there were other persons designated for that work. But he continued. My uncle Shami said, 'He just repaying a favour.' My grandfather silenced him with harsh words spoken in Hindi; it sounded like something obscene to me.

One day I saw the man looking intently at a picture of a Hindu Goddess with multiple arms and wondered about his infirmity and how he had arrived at that state. I knew that he was not really a sadhu, and this was not because he lacked piety or mystical powers — that earlier image of sadhus had shifted when I discovered that the silent and impressively impassive demeanour that they displayed was really just a kind of involuntary humility. They were, in the eyes of their benefactors, merely objects to be fed, clothed and temporarily housed; anything else was redundant, a position that they seemed to understand.

He was standing there, holding his leatherette pouch, resting his slight frame against his walking stick. A little girl, running, tripped against a protruding chair-leg and fell. I saw the walking stick being levered upright but the girl got up and ran off. He looked at the small, departing figure, then sat down on one of the chairs, his head bowed, propped against the stick. Above his head, the wind ruffled the crepe paper and the gossamery coquillage sprang to life; the gods and goddesses seemed to be flying away.

My mother said, 'It look like he meditating.'

Shami said provokingly, 'Everybody better watch out. Just now he might go in a trance.'

'Why you don't shut up,' my mother said.

Shami said, 'Why you vex for? He is just a occasional sadhu.'

From the corner of the stage, a very old sadhu — who had not shifted away from his corner since his arrival — was staring at the object of my uncle's amusement with a rigid unflinching expression. With his eyes fixed, he scratched his head, with long, slow, strokes.

The image is still vivid. Two old men, one mottled with age and looking like a decaying, neglected, ancient statue and the other not quite fitting into any role at that point, other than as a silent sweeper, cloistered within his distant secrets.

During the rest of that day — the final day — he tended to the singhasan where the pundits and the singers sat, removing the wilted flowers, wiping away the dust from the fragile styrotex temples that housed the miniature idols, reaching up with his walking stick and rearranging the mango leaves strung on nylon twine which criss-crossed the stage.

'First time them god and them getting so much attention,' Shami remarked.

And then the night. I have thought several times of that night and the following morning. Sometimes a memory is made sharper, given depth and focus through some simple incident that cannot be shunted aside, that prevents the memory from dissipating into fragments of forgotten things. I believe that had it not been for this final night, the events associated with this occasional sadhu — his humiliation in the drugstore, his sitting on the pavement, his clearing and sweeping — would have been lost. I sometimes wonder if I have inserted pieces of drama into this recollection, but I am certain this is not the case, because the events have stiffened in my mind and I see them as if they had happened yesterday. I see the pundit wiping his face with a saffron cloth, shifting, easing the strain on his knees, relieved perhaps that his week-long task had ended, I see the sadhus and Brahmins seated on the singhasan, tucking away the money they had been given somewhere within the folds of their dhotis. I see my father approaching the end of his interminable vote of thanks, speaking about someone who had, in spite of his ailment, ensured that the place was 'clean and pure,' and then calling that person to the microphone. And I see him reluctantly and awkwardly emerging from the unlit part of the stage, holding a dwarf palmiste palm for support. And then, that moment of uncertainty when he just stood there, with his head bowed, holding the microphone.

Then he sang his song. The voice, quivering, too high perhaps at first, then settling, smoothing out, arriving at a harmony with the mood of the congregation, being lowered to a fluting whisper, then gathering momentum and strength and rising with the burning cedar and incense smoke to permeate the hanging decorations and echo through the bamboo canopies. His bhajan

THE OCCASIONAL SADHU

gave energy to the harmonium player swaying over the wooden instrument, to the boy beating the drum, his fast hands barely visible, to the sadhus and brahmins, bestirred and watching with confusion and anxiety.

It may seem simple described like this — a talented singer energising his audience — but there was something else. I had never been enthralled by the mournful bhajans that I had heard at religious ceremonies but that night the song took me to ancient crumbling temples, to vines entwined over dusty statues, to a scorching sun and bodies writhing in pain and in pleading, to an unnatural and frenzied joy bubbling and bursting within all this degradation and despair — and I knew it was a joy linked more to a fixed fatalism than to any notion of reality. It took me to a past I had not known and to a belief of which I had only seen the fringes.

The following morning I saw him sitting on the edge of the stage, putting on his wooden sapats. His leatherette pouch was fixed beneath his arms; he looked about to leave, and in the lethargic tranquillity that marked the end of the Ramayan Yagna, his performance of the previous night was already half-forgotten. My father, who had awakened early that morning to supervise the removal of the hired folding chairs, asked him, 'You leaving?'

From somewhere in the gallery, my grandfather shouted, 'The van didn't come for the chairs yet?'

I answered, 'No, but the sadhu mister who sing last night leaving.'

I heard my mother's voice, 'Tell him to wait. I packing some things in a bag for him.'

My grandfather came down the steps, walking slowly and breathing heavily. He lowered himself on to the stage. 'So you sweep out and clean out already?'

'He up since five o'clock,' my father said.

My grandfather observed the pouch secreted beneath his arm. 'Don't go yet. They packing up a few things for you.'

The man looked disturbed. I saw him removing his pouch from beneath his arm and passing his finger along the zipper.

I asked him, 'So what you have in that case?'

'Go in the back and play,' my grandfather said angrily, words he had used to register his displeasure for as long as I can remember. 'Always playing the fool.'

But I was saved. My mother came out with the bag containing clothes, rice, potatoes, and perhaps money.

'This is my whole life right here, son. Everything.' His fingers caressed the pouch as if it was a living thing.

It was the first time I heard him speak and I was surprised at the briskness of his voice. I remember seeing a pained, childlike expression flickering briefly and I saw then that he was not as old as I had previously thought. His finger ran irresolutely along the zipper and then he opened it and withdrew a piece of glossy paper and held it towards me. My mother peered over my shoulder. It was a photograph of a young man, laughing, his teeth exposed and a little girl seated on his left leg. She had two bow clips in her hair and she was looking at the photographer with a distraught, rueful half-smile.

'I was about thirty years old then,' he said.

'That is you?' My mother took the photograph from my hand, a muted look of disbelief on her face. 'But all this jacket and tie? And who is the little girl?'

He gave me another photograph. It was of the same little girl, older now, but with the same rueful expression.

'Ooh! Look how pretty she come out!' my mother said.

Then, so many questions to ask, so many things to remove from formed impressions. I tried to connect the bearded face with the pictures. My grandfather, looking at the first photograph, said slowly, 'Yes. Is you really. But you looking well-off.' The unstated part of the question lingered. He took out then a folded and browning newspaper clipping. I read. It dealt with a young insurance salesman who had been involved in a road accident and who, after lying unconscious for thirteen days in the hospital, miraculously survived. Other photographs were produced, other letters and accounts, each relating some episode in his life, each in order, and this sequence told me that he had gone over the story of his life — contained in that leatherette pouch — many times.

After the accident, he had lost the use of his left leg and was unable to work. He began drinking, his earlier life faded, though the periodic memories of the life he had lost brought a despair which could only be displaced by further drinking. Then he was alone, drifting, barely surviving, living on the pavements.

To a fifteen year old his story was unreal. Later, I discovered that, in our island, the gap between pavement and power was not so wide and that far more people than I had previously imagined had made this journey.

I asked him, 'You have no family left?'

He pointed at the photograph of the little girl. 'She ... this is my daughter'

'She dead now?'

'No, son. She living somewhere up in Canada.'

'You never try to contact her,' my father asked.

He began to cry. I was glad that I had not asked the question. I looked at my grandfather's face.

My father said, 'Is okay. Is okay. She must be big now.'

He wiped his eyes with his merino. 'Yes she big now. And she don't want to see me again.'

'And what about your wife?' my mother asked.

'She is all I have,' he said resolutely, tracing his fingers over the picture of the little girl. All I have and she don't know whether I living or dead.' After a while he added, 'And she don't care.'

We asked him to stay. My grandfather offered him a job in the rice-mill, but he insisted on leaving. Later, in the inevitable family discussion, my mother said sadly, shaking her head and clacking her tongue, 'He didn't want to get too attach. That is why he had to leave. He living off his loneliness now.' It made sense then and it makes sense now.

I never saw him after that and now I don't know whether he is dead or still living on the pavements, moving from place to place. But a few days ago, I read an article in the *Sunday Guardian* and I thought of him. The article dealt with a Trinidad-born anthropologist attached to a Canadian university, who had received an award for some research she had recently done. Next to the article was a photograph of the woman, her poise and assurance barely masking a rueful half-smile.

ABOUT THE AUTHOR

Rabindranath Maharaj writes:

I was born in the small rural district of Tableland in South Trinidad. I attended the local Hindu school where my father was the principal; at ten years I left Tableland to attend Naparima College. For some time I stayed at San Fernando, about twenty miles from my home. Thereafter I did a B.A., M.A. and a Diploma in Education, all in English and all at U.W.I., St. Augustine. Most of my adult life has been spent as a secondary school teacher.

I have been writing for a very long time (since my primary school days actually). But writing, whenever it occurred, was mainly a personal thing and there was very little thought of publication. However, while at U.W.I. I wrote some stories which were received in such a way as I was encouraged to think of publication and persuaded of the futility of thinking only in terms of a private audience.

Many of the characters I have presented in my stories have been woven out of actual persons. My hometown, Tableland, like many small villages, possesses a wealth of characters, situations and incidents. But Trinidad itself is a good place for writers; everything here is mixed together – humour, racial tensions, oral traditions, political intrigues and even coups.

Praise for Rabindranath Maharaj's first published collection of stories, *The Interloper* (Canada: Goose Lane Editions, 1995):

'This book is wonderful!... The individual stories are rich and captivating. The whole is remarkable. Rabindranath Maharaj is a first-rate writer who deserves a wide readership and high acclaim.' – *The Halifax Chronicle*

The Interloper, with much humour, clarity, and sympathy, presents issues that affect us all. Maharaj does this through the creation of characters and various situations that are more true to life than they are fictitious.' – *Pride Magazine*

'He deals mainly with the immigrant experience, but these are more than simply tales of racism and wounded egos. They are complex explorations of the subject of home and displacement at multiple levels, including those of white Canadians who feel forced to adjust to what they perceive as "one stranger among many". Although these are dark tales, the collection is enlivened by wit and humour and layered, expressive language.'
Olive Senior, *Quill and Quire*

The author... knows how to capture the excitement, nostalgia, hope, terror, the self-consciousness of the outsider and expresses it vividly in the characters he creates. But however sympathetic he may be, he is also aware of the human frailties which burden them wherever they go.' – *The Daily Gleaner*

'An uninhibited look at cultural friction between Canadians and West Indians, and a surprising read in an era of political correctness.' – *Atlantic Books Today*

Peepal Tree Press publishes a wide selection of outstanding fiction, poetry, drama, history and literary criticism with a focus on the Caribbean, Africa, the South Asian diaspora and Black life in Britain. Peepal Tree is now the largest independent publisher of Caribbean writing in the world. All our books are high quality original paperbacks designed to stand the test of time and repeated readings.

All Peepal Tree books should be available through your local bookseller, though you are most welcome to place orders direct with us. When ordering a book direct from us, simply tell us the title, author, quantity and the address to which the book should be mailed. Please enclose a cheque or money order for the cover price of the book, plus 55p towards postage and packing.

Peepal Tree produces a yearly catalogue which gives current prices in sterling, US and Canadian dollars and full details of all our books. Write, phone or fax for your free copy.

You can contact Peepal Tree direct at:

17 King's Avenue
Leeds LS6 1QS
United Kingdom

tel: 44 (0)113 245 1703
fax: 44 (0)113 246 8368